THE FAR SIDE OF TIME

THE FAR SIDE
OF TIME
Thirteen Original Stories

A SCIENCE FICTION ANTHOLOGY
EDITED BY ROGER ELWOOD

808.83

Dodd, Mead & Company . New York

1974   235p

SF

ISBN: 0–396–06857–X
Library of Congress Catalog Card Number: 73–9272
Printed in the United States of America
by The Haddon Craftsmen, Inc., Scranton, Penna.

1. Science fiction
2. Short stories
I. Elwood, Roger

*To Virgina Kidd, a dear friend
and important influence*

CONTENTS

FOREWORD

Science fiction is an imaginative genre; without imagination—pure and unleashed—science fiction would would wither and die. Of course, imagination is involved in every creative writing endeavor, but this is doubly the case with science fiction; even mainstream authors are bound by the past and the present, but science fiction gives us the future whether by logical extrapolation or wild fantasy.

In the past, much of science fiction fell into a preconceived format, dominated by old-fashioned techniques; but, today, new wave influences and interest in social commentary have forced quite a bit of modern science fiction into plots that have little relation to those of the "old days."

But, still, traditional stories are being written—and yet most of these are traditional only in *form:* few if any have bug-eyed monsters. While they each have a beginning, a middle and an end, their plots are hardly "space opera."

THE FAR SIDE OF TIME is comprised of a fairly wide range of story types—the authors were given only one suggestion: Write stories you honestly *want* to do, stories that give you pleasure, as authors.

Included in this anthology are quite new authors; those

who are beyond the beginner stage; and professional authors with reputations going back many years.

In the first group are Gail Kimberly, Jay C. Haldeman II, and Nancy Mackenroth. I can't say that I "discovered" Mr. Haldeman, but Ms. Kimberly and Ms. Mackenroth have been published in my anthologies prior to their sales elsewhere.

In the second group are Gordon Eklund and Dennis O'-Neill: both fine authors and certain for wide recognition as time passes.

In the final group are Robert Silverberg, Barry Malzberg, John Brunner, Fritz Leiber, Ben Bova, Gene Wolfe, Raymond F. Jones, and Lloyd Biggle, Jr.; the awards they have won would fill several shelves indeed. [Malzberg and Silverberg won first and second place, respectively, in the initial John W. Campbell, Jr. Awards.]

The stories range from those noteworthy for sheer technique, as "The Capricorn Games," to those that are solidly and evocatively constructed, as "Flauna." Short-shorts ["Annie Mae," "Cues"], a short novel ["An Eye for an Eye"], medium-lengths ["Waif," "Slugging It Out," et cetera]—all are represented herein. Quality and diversity—these are the two key words for the stories in THE FAR SIDE OF TIME.

ROGER ELWOOD

THE FAR SIDE OF TIME

CAPRICORN GAMES
Robert Silverberg

Nikki stepped into the conical field of the ultrasonic cleanser, wriggling so that the unheard droning out of the machine's stubby snout could more effectively shear her skin of dead epidermal tissue, globules of dried sweat, dabs of yesterday's scents, and other debris; after three minutes she emerged, clean, bouncy, ready for the party. She programmed her party outfit: green buskins, lemon-yellow tunic of gauzy film, pale orange cape soft as a clam's mantle, and nothing underneath but Nikki, smooth glistening satiny Nikki. Her body was tuned and fit. The party was in her honor, though she was the only one who knew that. Today was her birthday, the 7th of January, 1999, twenty-four years old, no sign yet of bodily decay. Old Steiner had gathered an extraordinary assortment of guests: he promised to display a reader of minds, a billionaire, an authentic Byzantine duke, an Arab rabbi, a man who had married his own daughter, and other marvels. All of these, of course, subordinate to the true guest of honor, the evening's prize, the real birthday boy, the lion of the season, the celebrated Nicholson, who had lived a thousand years and who said he could help others to do the same. Nikki . . . Nicholson. Happy assonance, portending close harmony. You will show me, dear Nicholson, how I can live forever and never grow old. A cozy, soothing idea.

The sky beyond the sleek curve of her window was black, snow-dappled; she imagined she could hear the rusty howl of the wind and feel the sway of the frost-gripped building, ninety stories high. This was the worst winter she had ever known. Snow fell almost every day, a planetary snow, a global shiver, not even sparing the tropics. Ice hard as iron bands bound the streets of New York. Walls were slippery, the air had a cutting edge. Tonight Jupiter gleamed fiercely in the blackness like a diamond in a raven's forehead. Thank God she didn't have to go outside. She could wait out the winter within this tower. The mail came by pneumatic tube. The penthouse restaurant fed her. She had friends on a dozen floors. The building was a world, warm, snug. Let it snow. Let the sour gales come. Nikki checked herself in the all-around mirror: very nice; very, very nice. Sweet filmy yellow folds. Hint of thigh, hint of breasts. More than a hint when there's a light-source behind her. She glowed. Fluffed her short glossy black hair. Dab of scent. Everyone loved her. Beauty is a magnet: repels some, attracts many, leaves no one unmoved. It was nine o'clock.

"Upstairs," she said to the elevator. "Steiner's place."

"Eighty-eighth floor," the elevator said.

"I know that. You're so sweet."

Music in the hallway: Mozart, crystalline and sinuous. The door to Steiner's apartment was a half-barrel of chromed steel, like the entrance to a bank vault. Nikki smiled into the scanner. The barrel revolved. Steiner held his hands like cups, centimeters from her chest, by way of greeting. "Beautiful," he murmured.

"So glad you asked me to come."

"Practically everybody's here already. It's a wonderful party, love."

She kissed his shaggy cheek. In October they had met in

the elevator. He was past sixty and looked less than forty. When she touched his body, she perceived it as an object encased in milky ice, like a mammoth fresh out of the Siberian permafrost. They had been lovers for two weeks. Autumn had given way to winter and Nikki had passed out of his life, but he had kept his word about the parties: here she was, invited.

"Alexius Ducas," said a short, wide man with a dense black beard, parted in the middle. He bowed. A good flourish. Steiner evaporated and she was in the keeping of the Byzantine duke. He maneuvered her at once across the thick white carpet to a place where clusters of spotlights, sprouting like angry fungi from the wall, revealed the contours of her body. Others turned to look. Duke Alexius favored her with a heavy stare. But she felt no excitement. Byzantium had been over for a long time. He brought her a goblet of chilled green wine and said, "Are you ever in the Aegean Sea? My family has its ancestral castle on an island eighteen kilometers east of—"

"Excuse me, but which is the man named Nicholson?"

"Nicholson is merely the name he currently uses. He claims to have had a shop in Constantinople during the reign of my ancestor the Basileus Manuel Comnenus." A patronizing click, tongue on teeth. "Only a shopkeeper." The Byzantine eyes sparkled ferociously. "How beautiful you are!"

"Which one is he?"

"There. By the couch."

Nikki saw only a wall of backs. She tilted to the left and peered. No use. She would get to him later. Alexius Ducas continued to offer her his body with his eyes. She whispered languidly, "Tell me all about Byzantium."

He got as far as Constantine the Great before he bored her. She finished her wine and, coyly extending the glass, persuaded a smooth young man passing by to refill it for her. The Byzantine looked sad. "The empire then was divided," he said, "among—"

"This is my birthday," she announced.

"Yours also? My congratulations. Are you as old as—"

"Not nearly. Not by half. I won't even be five hundred for some time," she said, and turned to take her glass. The smooth young man did not wait to be captured. The party engulfed him like an avalanche. Sixty, eighty guests, all in motion. The draperies were pulled back, revealing the full fury of the snowstorm. No one was watching it. Steiner's apartment was like a movie set: great porcelain garden stools, Ming or even Sung, walls painted with flat sheets of bronze and scarlet, pre-Columbian artifacts in spotlit niches, sculptures like aluminum spiderwebs, Dürer etchings, the loot of the ages. Squat shaven-headed servants, Mayas or Khmers or perhaps Olmecs, circulated impassively offering trays of delicacies: caviar, sea urchins, bits of roasted meat, tiny sausages, burritos in startling chili sauce. Hands darted unceasingly from trays to lips. This was a gathering of life-eaters, world-swallowers. Duke Alexius was stroking her arm. "I will leave at midnight," he said gently. "It would be a delight if you left with me."

"I have other plans," she told him.

"Even so." He bowed courteously, outwardly undisappointed. "Possibly another time. My card?" It appeared as if by magic in his hand: a sliver of tawny cardboard, elaborately engraved. She put it in her purse and the room swallowed him. Instantly a big, wild-eyed man took his place before her. "You've never heard of me," he began.

"Is that a boast or an apology?"

"I'm quite ordinary. I work for Steiner. He thought it would be amusing to invite me to one of his parties."

"What do you do?"

"Invoices and debarkations. Isn't this an amazing place?"

"What's your sign?" Nikki asked him.

"Libra."

"I'm Capricorn. Tonight's my birthday as well as *his*. If you're really Libra, you're wasting your time with me. Do you have a name?"

"Martin Bliss."

"Nikki."

"There isn't any Mrs. Bliss, hah-hah."

Nikki licked her lips. "I'm hungry. Would you get me some canapés?"

She was gone as soon as he moved toward the food. Circumnavigating the long room, past the string quintet, past the bartender's throne, past the window, until she had a good view of the man called Nicholson. He didn't disappoint her. He was slender, supple, not tall, strong in the shoulders. A man of presence and authority. She wanted to put her lips to him and suck immortality out. His head was a flat triangle, brutal cheekbones, thin lips, dark mat of curly hair, no beard, no mustache. His eyes were keen, electric, intolerably wise. He must have seen everything twice, at the very least. Nikki had read his book. Everyone had. He had been a king, a lama, a slave-trader, a slave. Always taking pains to conceal his implausible longevity, now offering his terrible secret freely to the members of the Book-of-the-Month Club. Why had he chosen to surface and reveal himself? Because this is the necessary moment of revelation, he had said. When he must stand forth as what he is, so that he might impart his gift to others, lest he lose it. Lest he lose it. At the stroke of the new century he must share his prize of life. A dozen people surrounded him, catching his glow. He glanced through a palisade of shoulders and locked his eyes on hers; Nikki felt impaled, exalted, chosen. Warmth spread through her loins like a river of molten tungsten, like a stream of hot honey. She started to go to him. A corpse got in her way. Death's-head, parchment skin, nightmare eyes. A scaly hand brushed her bare biceps. A frightful eroded voice croaked, "How old do you think I am?"

"Oh, God!"

"How old?"

"Two thousand?"

"I'm fifty-eight. I won't live to see fifty-nine. Here, smoke one of these."

With trembling hands he offered her a tiny ivory tube. There was a Gothic monogram near one end—FXB—and a translucent green capsule at the other. She pressed the capsule and a flickering blue flame sprouted. She inhaled. "What is it?" she asked.

"My own mixture. Soma Number Five. You like it?"

"I'm smeared," she said. "Absolutely smeared. Oh, God!" The walls were flowing. The snow had turned to tinfoil. An instant hit. The corpse had a golden halo. Dollar signs rose into view like stigmata on his furrowed forehead. She heard the crash of the surf, the roar of the waves. The deck was heaving. The masts were cracking. Woman overboard, she cried, and heard her inaudible voice disappearing down a tunnel of echoes, boingg boingg boingg. She clutched at his frail wrists. "You bastard, what did you *do* to me?"

"I'm Francis Xavier Byrne."

Oh. The billionaire. Byrne Industries, the great conglomerate. Steiner had promised her a billionaire tonight.

"Are you going to die soon?" she asked.

"No later than Easter. Money can't help me now. I'm a walking metastasis." He opened his ruffled shirt. Something bright and metallic, like chain mail, covered his chest. "Life-support system," he confided. "It operates me. Take it off for half an hour and I'd be finished. Are you a Capricorn?"

"How did you know?"

"I may be dying, but I'm not stupid. You have the Capricorn gleam in your eyes. What am I?"

She hesitated. His eyes were gleaming, too. Self-made man, fantastic business sense, energy, arrogance. Capricorn, of course. No, too easy. "Leo," she said.

"No. Try again." He pressed another monogramed tube into her hand and strode away. She hadn't yet come down from the last one, although the most flamboyant effects had ebbed. Party guests swirled and flowed around her. She no longer could see Nicholson. The snow seemed to be turning to hail, little hard particles spattering the vast windows and leaving white abraded tracks: or were her perceptions merely sharper? The roar of conversation seemed to rise and fall as if someone were adjusting a volume control. The lights fluctuated in a counterpointed rhythm. She felt dizzy. A tray of golden cocktails went past her and she hissed, "Where's the bathroom?"

Down the hall. Five strangers clustered outside it, talking in scaly whispers. She floated through them, grabbed the sink's cold edge, thrust her face to the oval concave mirror. A death's-head. Parchment skin, nightmare eyes. No! No! She blinked and her own features reappeared. Shivering, she made an effort to pull herself together. The medicine cabinet held a tempting collection of drugs, Steiner's all-purpose remedies. Without looking at labels, Nikki seized a handful of vials and gobbled pills at random. A flat red one, a tapering green one, a succulent yellow gelatin capsule. Maybe headache remedies, maybe hallucinogens. Who knows, who cares? We Capricorns are not always as cautious as you think.

Someone knocked at the bathroom door. She answered

and found the bland, hopeful face of Martin Bliss hovering near the ceiling. Eyes protruding faintly, cheeks florid. "They said you were sick. Can I do anything for you?" So kind, so sweet. She touched his arm, grazed his cheek with her lips. Beyond him in the hall stood a broad-bodied man with close-cropped blond hair, glacial blue eyes, a plump perfect face. His smile was intense and brilliant. "That's easy," he said. "Capricorn."

"Can you guess my—" She stopped, stunned. "Sign?" she finished, voice very small. "How did you do that? Oh."

"Yes. I'm that one."

She felt more than naked, stripped down to the ganglia, to the synapses. "What's the trick?"

"No trick. I listen. I hear."

"You hear people thinking?"

"More or less. Do you think it's a party game?" He was beautiful but terrifying, like a samurai sword in motion. She wanted him but she didn't dare. He's got my number, she thought. I would never have any secrets from him. He said sadly, "I don't mind that. I know I frighten a lot of people. Some don't care."

"What's your name?"

"Tom," he said. "Hello, Nikki."

"I feel very sorry for you."

"Not really. You can kid yourself, if you need to. But you can't kid me. Anyway, you don't sleep with men you feel sorry for."

"I don't sleep with you."

"You will," he said.

"I thought you were just a mind reader. They didn't tell me you did prophecies, too."

He leaned close and smiled. The smile demolished her. She had to fight to keep from falling. "I've got your number, all right," he said in a low harsh voice. "I'll call you next Tuesday." As he walked away, he said, "You're wrong. I'm a Virgo. Believe it or not."

Nikki returned, numb, to the living room. "—the figure of the mandala," Nicholson was saying. His voice was dark, focused, a pure basso cantante. "The essential thing that every mandala has is a center: the place where everything is born, the eye of God's mind, the heart of darkness and of light, the core of the storm. All right: you must move toward the center, find the vortex at the boundary of yang and yin, place yourself right at the mandala's midpoint. *Center yourself.* Do you follow the metaphor? Center yourself at *now,* the eternal *now.* To move off center is to move forward toward death, backward toward birth, always the fatal polar swings; but if you're capable of positioning yourself constantly at the focus of the mandala, right on center, you have access to the fountain of renewal, you become an organism capable of constant self-healing, constant self-replenishment, constant expansion into regions beyond self. Do you follow? The power of—"

Steiner, at her elbow, said tenderly, "How beautiful you are in the first moments of erotic fixation."

"It's a marvelous party."

"Are you meeting interesting people?"

"Is there any other kind?" she asked.

Nicholson abruptly detached himself from the circle of his audience and strode across the room, alone, in a quick decisive knight's-move toward the bar. Nikki, hurrying to intercept him, collided with a shaven-headed tray-bearing servant. The tray slid smoothly from the man's thick fingertips and launched itself into the air like a spinning shield; a rainfall of skewered meat in an oily green curry sauce spattered the white carpet. The servant was utterly motionless. He stood frozen like some sort of Mexican stone idol, thick-necked, flat-nosed, for a long painful moment; then he turned his head slowly to the left and regretfully contemplated his rigid outspread hand, shorn of its tray; finally he swung his head toward Nikki, and his expressionless granite face took on for a quick flickering instant a look of total hatred, a coruscating emanation of contempt and disgust that faded immediately. He laughed: hu-hu-hu, a neighing snicker. His superiority was overwhelming. Nikki floundered in quicksands of humiliation. Hastily she escaped, a zig and a zag, around the tumbled goodies and across to the bar. Nicholson, still by himself. Her face went crimson. She felt short of breath. Hunting for words, tongue all thumbs. Finally, in a catapulting blurt: "Happy birthday!"

"Thank you," he said solemnly.

"Are you enjoying your birthday?"

"Very much."

"I'm amazed that they don't bore you. I mean, having had so many of them."

"I don't bore easily." He was awesomely calm, drawing on some bottomless reservoir of patience. He gave her a look that was at the same time warm and impersonal. "I find everything interesting," he said.

"That's curious. I said more or less the same thing to Steiner just a few minutes ago. You know, it's my birthday, too."

"Really?"

"The seventh of January, 1975, for me."

"Hello, 1975. I'm—" He laughed. "It sounds absolutely absurd, doesn't it?"

"—the seventh of January, 982."

"You've been doing your homework."

"I've read your book," she said. "Can I make a silly remark? My God, you don't *look* like you're a thousand and seventeen years old."

"How should I look?"

"More like him," she said, indicating Francis Xavier Byrne.

Nicholson chuckled. She wondered if he liked her. Maybe. Maybe. Nikki risked some eye contact. He was hardly a centimeter taller than she was, which made it a terrifyingly intimate experience. He regarded her steadily, centeredly; she imagined a throbbing mandala surrounding him, luminous turquoise spokes emanating from his heart, radiant red and green spiderweb rings connecting them. Reaching from her loins, she threw a loop of desire around him. Her eyes were explicit. His were veiled. She felt him calmly retreating. Take me inside, she pleaded; take me to one of the back rooms. Pour life into me. She said, "How will you choose the people you're going to instruct in the secret?"

"Intuitively."

"Refusing anybody who asks directly, of course."

"Refusing anybody who asks."

"Did *you* ask?"

"You said you read my book."

"Oh. Yes. I remember: you didn't know what was happening, you didn't understand anything until it was over."

"I was a simple lad," he said. "That was a long time ago." His eyes were alive again. He's drawn to me. He sees that I'm his kind, that I deserve him. Capricorn, Capricorn, Capricorn, you and me, he-goat and she-goat. Play my game, Cap. "How are you named?" he asked.

"Nikki."

"A beautiful name. A beautiful woman."

The emptiness of the compliments devastated her. She

realized she had arrived with mysterious suddenness at a necessary point of tactical withdrawal; retreat was obligatory, lest she push too hard and destroy the tenuous contact so tensely established. She thanked him with a glance and gracefully slipped away, pivoting toward Martin Bliss, slipping her arm through his. Bliss quivered at the gesture, glowed, leaped into a higher energy state. She resonated to his vibrations, going up and up. She was at the heart of the party, the center of the mandala: standing flatfooted, legs slightly apart, making her body a polar axis, with lines of force zooming up out of the earth, up through the basement levels of this building, up the eighty-eight stories of it, up through her sex, her heart, her head. This is how it must feel, she thought, when undyingness is conferred on you. A moment of spontaneous grace, the kindling of an inner light. She looked love at poor sappy Bliss. You dear heart, you dumb walking pun. The string quintet made molten sounds. "What is that?" she asked. "Brahms?" Bliss offered to find out. Alone, she was vulnerable to Francis Xavier Byrne, who brought her down with a single cadaverous glance.

"Have you guessed it yet?" he asked. "The sign."

She stared through his ragged cancerous body, blazing with decomposition. "Scorpio," she told him hoarsely.

"Right! Right!" He pulled a pendant from his breast and draped its golden chain over her head. "For you," he rasped, and fled. She fondled it. A smooth green stone. Jade? Emerald? Lightly engraved on its domed face was the looped cross, the crux ansata. Beautiful. The gift of life, from the dying man. She waved fondly to him across a forest of heads and winked. Bliss returned.

"They're playing something by Schönberg," he reported. *"Verklärte Nacht."*

"How lovely." She flipped the pendant and let it fall back

against her breasts. "Do you like it?"

"I'm sure you didn't have it a moment ago."

"It sprouted," she told him. She felt high, but not as high as she had been just after leaving Nicholson. That sense of herself as focal point had departed. The party seemed chaotic. Couples were forming, dissolving, re-forming; shadowy figures were stealing away in twos and threes toward the bedrooms; the servants were more obsessively thrusting their trays of drinks and snacks at the remaining guests; the hail had reverted to snow, and feathery masses silently struck the windows, sticking there, revealing their glistening mandalic structures for painfully brief moments before they deliquesced. Nikki struggled to regain her centered position. She indulged in a cheering fantasy: Nicholson coming to her, formally touching her cheek, telling her, "You will be one of the elect." In less than twelve months the time would come for him to gather with his seven still unnamed disciples to see in the new century, and he would take their hands into his hands, he would pump the vitality of the undying into their bodies, sharing with them the secret that had been shared with him a thousand years ago. Who? Who? Who? Me. Me. Me. But where had Nicholson gone? His aura, his glow, that cone of imaginary light that had appeared to surround him—nowhere. A man in a lacquered orange wig began furiously to quarrel, almost under Nikki's nose, with a much younger woman wearing festoons of bioluminescent pearls. Man and wife, evidently. They were both sharp-featured, with glossy, protuberant eyes, rigid faces, cheek-muscles working intensely. Live together long enough, come to look alike. Their dispute had a stale, ritualistic flavor, as though they had staged it all too many times before: they were explaining to each other the events that had caused the quarrel, interpreting them, recapitulating them, shading them, justifying, attacking, de-

CAPRICORN GAMES   13

fending—you said this because and that led me to respond that way because, no, on the contrary I said this because you said that—all of it in a quiet screechy tone, sickening, agonizing, pure death. "He's her biological father," a man next to Nikki said. "She was one of the first of the in vitro babies, and he was the donor, and five years ago he tracked her down and married her. A loophole in the law." Five years? They sounded as if they had been married for fifty. Walls of pain and boredom encased them. Only their eyes were alive. Nikki found it impossible to imagine those two in bed, bodies entwined in the act of love. Act of love, she thought, and laughed. Where was Nicholson? Duke Alexius, flushed and sweat-beaded, bowed to her. "I will leave soon," he announced, and she received the announcement gravely but without reacting, as though he had merely commented on the fluctuations of the storm, or had spoken in Greek. He bowed again and went away. Nicholson? Nicholson? She grew calm again, finding her center. He will come to me when he is ready. There was contact between us, and it was real and good.

Bliss, beside her, gestured and said, "A rabbi of Syrian birth, formerly Muslim, highly regarded among Jewish theologians."

She nodded but didn't look.

"An astronaut just back from Mars. I've never seen anyone's skin tanned quite that color."

The astronaut held no interest for her. She worked at kicking herself back into high. The party was approaching a climactic moment, she felt, a time when commitments were being made and decisions taken. The clink of ice in glasses, the foggy vapors of psychedelic inhalants, the press of warm flesh all about her—she was wired into everything, she was alive and receptive, she was entering into the twitching hour, the hour of galvanic jerks. She grew wild and reckless. Impulsively she kissed Bliss, straining on tiptoes, jabbing her tongue deep into his startled mouth. Then she broke free. Someone was playing with the lights: they grew redder, then gained force and zoomed to blue-white ferocity. Far across the room a crowd was surging and billowing around the fallen figure of Francis Xavier Byrne, slumped loose-jointedly against the base of the bar. His eyes were open but glassy. Nicholson crouched over him, reaching into his shirt, making delicate adjustments of the controls of the chain-mail beneath. "It's all right," Steiner was saying. "Give him some air. It's all right!" Confusion. Hubbub. A torrent of tangled input.

"—they say there's been a permanent change in the weather patterns. Colder winters from now on, because of accumulations of dust in the atmosphere that screen the sun's rays. Until we freeze altogether by around the year 2200—"

"—but the carbon dioxide is supposed to start a greenhouse effect that's causing *warmer* weather, I thought, and—"

"—the proposal to generate electrical power from—"

"—the San Andreas fault—"

"—financed by debentures convertible into—"

"—capsules of botulism toxin—"

"—to be distributed at a ratio of one per thousand families, through Greenland and the Kamchatka Metropolitan Area—"

"—in the sixteenth century, when you could actually hope to found your own empire in some unknown part of the—"

"—unresolved conflicts of Capricorn personality—"

"—intense concentration and meditation upon the completed mandala so that the contents of the work are transferred to and identified with the mind and body of the beholder. I mean, technically, what occurs is the reabsorption of cosmic

CAPRICORN GAMES   15

forces. In the process of construction these forces—"

"—butterflies, which are no longer to be found anywhere in—"

"—were projected out from the chaos of the unconscious; in the process of absorption, the powers are drawn back in again—"

"—reflecting transformations of the DNA in the light-collecting organ, which—"

"—the snow—"

"—a thousand years, can you imagine that? And—"

"—her body—"

"—formerly a toad—"

"—just back from Mars, and there's that *look* in his eye—"

"Hold me," Nikki said. "Just hold me. I'm very dizzy."

"Would you like a drink?"

"Just hold me." She pressed against cool sweet-smelling fabric. His chest, unyielding beneath it. Steiner. Very male. He steadied her, but only for a moment. Other responsibilities summoned him. When he released her, she swayed. He beckoned to someone else, blond, soft-faced. The mind reader, Tom. Passing her along the chain from man to man.

"You feel better now," the telepath told her.

"Are you positive of that?"

"Very."

"Can you read any mind in the room?" she asked.

He nodded.

"Even *his?*"

Again a nod. "He's the clearest of all. He's been using it so long, all the channels are worn deep."

"Then he really is a thousand years old?"

"You didn't believe it?"

Nikki shrugged. "Sometimes I don't know what I believe."

"He's *old.*"

"You'd be the one to know."

"He's a phenomenon. He's absolutely extraordinary." A pause, quick, stabbing. "Would you like to see into his mind?"

"How can I?"

"I'll patch you right in, if you'd like me to." The glacial eyes flashed sudden mischievous warmth. "Yes?"

"I'm not sure I want to."

"You're very sure. You're curious as hell. Don't kid me. Don't play games, Nikki. You want to see into him."

"Maybe." Grudgingly.

"You do. Believe me, you do. Here. Relax, let your shoulders slump a little, loosen up, make yourself receptive, and I'll establish the link."

"Wait," she said.

But it was too late. The mind reader serenely parted her consciousness like Moses doing the Red Sea, and rammed something into her forehead, something thick but insubstantial, a truncheon of fog. She quivered and recoiled. She felt violated. It was like her first time in bed, in that moment when all the fooling around at last was over, the kissing and the nibbling and the stroking, and suddenly there was this object deep inside her body. She had never forgotten that sense of being impaled. But of course it had been not only an intrusion but also a source of ecstasy. As was this. The object within her was the consciousness of Nicholson. In wonder she explored its surface, rigid and weathered, pitted with the myriad ablations of re-entry. Ran her trembling hands over its bronzy roughness. Remained outside it. Tom the mind reader gave her a nudge. Go on, go on. Deeper. Don't hold back. She folded herself around Nicholson and drifted into him like ectoplasm seeping into sand. Suddenly she lost her bearings. The discreet and impermeable boundary marking the end of her self and the beginning of his became indistinct. It was impossible to distinguish between her experiences and his, nor could she separate the pulsations of her nervous system from the impulses traveling along his. Phantom memories assailed and engulfed her. She was transformed into a node of pure perception, a steady cool isolated eye, surveying and recording. Images flashed. She was toiling upward along a dazzling snowy crest, with jagged Himalayan fangs hanging above her in the white sky and a warm-muzzled yak snuffling wearily at her side. A platoon of swarthy-skinned little men accompanied her, slanty eyes, heavy coats, thick boots. The stink of rancid butter, the cutting edge of an impossible wind: and there, gleaming in the sudden sunlight, a pile of fire-bright yellow plaster with a thousand winking windows, a building, a lamasery strung along a mountain ridge. The nasal sound of distant horns and trumpets. The hoarse chanting of lotus-legged monks. What were they chanting? Om? Om? Om! *Om,* and flies buzzed around her nose, and she lay hunkered in a flimsy canoe, coursing silently down a midnight river in the heart of Africa, drowning in humidity. Brawny naked men with purple-black skins crouching close. Sweaty fronds dangling from flamboyantly excessive shrubbery; the snouts of crocodiles rising out of the dark water like toothy flowers; great nauseous orchids blossoming high in the smooth-shanked trees. And on shore, five white men in Elizabethan costume, wide-brimmed hats, drooping sweaty collars, lace, fancy buckles, curling red beards. Errol Flynn as Sir Francis Drake, blunderbuss dangling in crook of arm. The white men laughing, beckoning, shouting to the men in the canoe. Am I slave or slavemaster? No answer. Only a blurring and a new vision: autumn leaves blowing across the open doorways of straw-thatched huts, shivering oxen crouched in bare stubble-strewn fields, grim long-mustachioed men with close-cropped hair riding diagonal courses toward the horizon. Crusaders, are they? Or warriors of Hungary on their way to meet the dread Mongols? Defenders of the imperiled Anglo-Saxon realm against the Norman invaders? They could be any of these. But always that steady cool eye, always that unmoving consciousness at the center of every scene. *Him,* eternal, all-enduring. And then: the train rolling westward, belching white smoke, the plains unrolling infinityward, the big brown fierce-eyed bison standing in shaggy clumps along the right-of-way, the man with turbulent shoulder-length hair laughing, slapping a twenty-dollar gold piece on the table, picking up his rifle—.50-caliber breech-loading Springfield—he aims casually through the door of the moving train, he squeezes off a shot, another, another. Three shaggy brown corpses beside the tracks, and the train rolls onward, honking raucously. Her arm and shoulder tingled with the impact of those shots. Then: a fetid waterfront, bales of cloves and peppers and cinnamon, small brown-skinned men in turbans and loincloths arguing under a terrible sun. Tiny irregular silver coins glittering in the palm of her hand. The jabber of some Malabar dialect counterpointed with fluid mocking Portuguese. Do we sail now with Vasco da Gama? Perhaps. And then a gray Teutonic street, wind-swept, medieval, bleak Lutheran faces scowling from leaded windows. And then the Gobi steppe, with horsemen and campfires and dark tents. And then New York City, unmistakably New York City, with square black automobiles scurrying between the stubby skyscrapers like glossy beetles, a scene out of some silent movie. And then. And then. Everywhere, everything, all times, all places, a discontinuous flow of events but always that clarity of vision, that rock-steady perception, that solid mind at the center, that unshakable identity, that unchanging self—

—with whom I am inextricably enmeshed—

There was no "I," there was no "he," there was only the one ever-perceiving point of view. But abruptly she felt a change of focus, a distancing effect, a separation of self and self, so that she was looking at him as he lived his many lives, seeing him from the outside, seeing him plainly changing identities as others might change clothing, growing beards and mustaches, shaving them, cropping his hair, letting his hair grow, adopting new fashions, learning languages, forging documents. She saw him in all his thousand years of guises and subterfuges, saw him real and unified and centered beneath his obligatory camouflages—

—and saw him seeing her—

Instantly contact broke. She staggered. Arms caught her. She pulled away from the smiling plump-faced blond man, muttering, "What have you done? You didn't tell me you'd show *me* to *him*."

"How else can there be a linkage?" the telepath asked.

"You didn't tell me. You should have told me." Everything was lost. She couldn't bear to be in the same room as Nicholson now. Tom reached for her, but she stumbled past him, stepping on people. They winked up at her. Someone stroked her leg. She forced her way through improbable raccoons, three women and two servants, five men and a tablecloth. A glass door, a gleaming silvery handle: she pushed. Out onto the terrace. The purity of the gale might cleanse her. Behind her, faint gasps, a few shrill screams, annoyed expostulations: "Close that thing!" She slammed it. Alone in the night, eighty-eight stories above street level, she offered herself to the storm. Her filmy tunic shielded her not at all. Snowflakes burned against her breasts. Her nipples hardened and rose like fiery beacons, jutting against the soft fabric. The snow stung her throat, her shoulders, her arms. Far below, the wind churned newly fallen crystals into spiral galaxies. The street was invisible. Thermal confusions brought updrafts that seized the edge of her tunic and whipped it outward from her body. Fierce cold particles of hail were driven into her bare pale thighs. She stood with her back to the party. Did anyone in there notice her? Would someone think she was contemplating suicide, and come rushing gallantly out to save her? Capricorns didn't commit suicide. They might threaten it, yes, they might even tell themselves quite earnestly that they were really going to do it, but it was only a game, only a game. No one came to her. She didn't turn. Gripping the railing, she fought to calm herself.

No use. Not even the bitter air could help. Frost in her eyelashes, snow on her lips. The pendant Byrne had given her blazed between her breasts. The air was white with a throbbing green underglow. It seared her eyes. She was off center and floundering. She felt herself still reverberating through the centuries, gonging back and forth across the orbit of Nicholson's interminable life. What year is this? Is it 1386, 1912, 1532, 1779, 1043, 1977, 1235, 1129, 1836? So many centuries. So many lives. And yet always the one true self, changeless, unchangeable.

Gradually the resonances died away. Nicholson's unending epochs no longer filled her mind with terrible noise. She began to shiver, not from fear but merely from cold, and tugged at her moist tunic, trying to shield her nakedness. Melting snow left hot clammy tracks across her breasts and belly. A halo of steam surrounded her. Her heart pounded.

She wondered if what she had experienced had been genuine contact with Nicholson's soul, or rather only some trick of Tom's, a simulation of contact. Was it possible, after all, even for Tom to create a linkage between two non-telepathic minds such as hers and Nicholson's? Maybe Tom had fabricated it all himself, using images borrowed from Nicholson's book.

In that case there might still be hope for her.

A delusion, she knew. A fantasy born of the desperate optimism of the hopeless. But nevertheless—

She found the handle, let herself back into the party. A gust accompanied her, sweeping snow inward. People stared. She was like death arriving at the feast. Doglike, she shook off the searing snowflakes. Her clothes were wet and stuck to her skin; she might as well have been naked. "You poor shivering thing," a woman said. She pulled Nikki into a tight embrace. It was the sharp-faced woman, the bulgy-eyed bottle-born one, bride of her own father. Her hands traveled swiftly over Nikki's body, caressing her breasts, touching her cheek, her forearm, her haunch. "Come inside with me," she crooned. "I'll make you warm." Her lips grazed Nikki's. A playful tongue sought hers. For a moment, needing the warmth, Nikki gave herself to the embrace. Then she pulled away. "No," she said. "Some other time. Please." Wriggling free, she started across the room. An endless journey. Like crossing the Sahara by pogo stick. Voices, faces, laughter. A dryness in her throat. Then she was in front of Nicholson.

Well. Now or never.

"I have to talk to you," she said.

"Of course." His eyes were merciless. No wrath in them, not even disdain, only an incredible patience more terrifying than anger or scorn. She would not let herself bend before that cool level gaze.

She said, "A few minutes ago, did you have an odd experience, a sense that someone was—well, looking into your mind? I know it sounds foolish, but—"

"Yes. It happened." So calm. How did he stay that close to his center? That unwavering eye, that uniquely self-contained self, perceiving all—the lamasery, the slave depot, the railroad train, everything, all time gone by, all time to come—how did he manage to be so tranquil? She knew she never could learn such calmness. She knew he knew it. He has my number, all right. She found that she was looking at his cheekbones, at his forehead, at his lips. Not into his eyes.

"You have the wrong image of me," she told him.

"It isn't an image," he said. "What I have is you."

"No."

"Face yourself, Nikki. If you can figure out where to look." He laughed. Gently, but she was demolished.

An odd thing, then. She forced herself to stare into his eyes and felt a snapping of awareness from one mode into some other and he turned into an old man. That mask of changeless early maturity dissolved and she saw the frightening yellowed eyes, the maze of furrows and gullies, the toothless gums, the drooling lips, the hollow throat, the self beneath the face. A thousand years, a thousand years! And every moment of those thousand years was visible. "You're old," she whispered. "You disgust me. I wouldn't want to be like you, not for anything!" She backed away, shaking. "An old, old, old man. All a masquerade!"

He smiled. "Isn't that pathetic?"

"Me or you? *Me or you?*"

He didn't answer. She was bewildered. When she was five paces away from him, there came another snapping of awareness, a second changing of phase, and suddenly he was himself again, taut-skinned, erect, appearing to be perhaps thirty-five years old. A globe of silence hung between them. The force of his rejection was withering. She summoned her last strength for a parting glare. *I didn't want you either, friend, not any single part of you.* He saluted cordially. Dismissal.

Martin Bliss, grinning vacantly, stood near the bar. "Let's go," she said savagely. "Take me home!"

"But—"

"It's just a few floors below." She thrust her arm through his. He blinked, shrugged, fell into step.

"I'll call you Tuesday, Nikki," Tom said as they swept past him.

Downstairs, on her home turf, she felt better. In the bedroom they quickly dropped their clothes. His body was pink, hairy, serviceable. She turned the bed on and it began to murmur and throb. "How old do you think I am?" she asked.

"Twenty-six?" Bliss said vaguely.

"Bastard!" She pulled him down on top of her. Her hands raked his skin. Her thighs parted. Go on. Like an animal, she thought. Like an animal! She was getting older moment by moment, she was dying in his arms.

"You're much better than I expected," she said eventually.

He looked down, baffled, amazed. "You could have chosen anyone at that party. Anyone."

"Almost anyone," she said.

When he was asleep, she slipped out of bed. Snow was still falling. She heard the thunk of bullets and the whine of wounded bison. She heard the clangor of swords on shields. She heard lamas chanting: Om, Om, Om. No sleep for her this night, none. The clock was ticking like a bomb. The century was flowing remorselessly toward its finish. She checked her face for wrinkles in the bathroom mirror. Smooth, smooth, all smooth under the blue fluorescent glow. Her eyes looked bloody. Her nipples were still hard. She took a little alabaster jar from one of the bathroom cabinets and three slender red capsules fell out of it, into her palm. Happy birthday, dear Nikki, happy birthday to you. She swallowed all three. Went back to bed. Waited, listening to the slap of snow on glass, for the visions to come and carry her away.

ANNIE MAE: A LOVE STORY
Dennis O'Neil

All day they had trudged the cold pavements of St. Louis, progressing from the elegance of the west end, through the lower middle class roughness of the Forest Park area, to the poverty of the north side. Finally, just as dusk was gathering and a chill November rain began to fall, they found a room they could afford. He paid the landlady, a fetid stick of a woman, and carefully counted his change, and both of them followed her up a steep flight of groaning stairs to a door on the top floor.

They went inside. There was a double bed, covered with a moth-ravaged blanket, and a cracked porcelain washstand, and a bloated old easy chair, stuffing the color of dirty snow bulging from the seams, and nothing else. It was cold. It was filthy.

First, she cried. Then they quarreled.

And later, they lay beneath the blanket, clinging together for warmth. He was afraid to speak, afraid even to mention their situation, for fear of more tears and argument. Yet neither could sleep. So he told her a story. A love story.

Which was:

How long ago?—forty thousand years, at least—he was CroMagnon, and unhappy. Shunned. Disliked. Despised by the tribe. Because he was an uncommonly fine hunter, though, he managed to eat, and because he wasn't as frightened as the rest, he found an excellent home, a snug cave halfway up a cliffside, accessible only by a series of tiny hand- and footholds. He lived in moderate peace, reasonable comfort, and vague discontent. He was hungry—he knew not for what. Certainly not meat—he had plenty. But for something.

One morning, he awoke as usual, thoroughly scratched himself, shouldered his weapon, and stepped into the sunlight. He surveyed the familiar scene: the curve of the cliffside, and the home of the tribe on the far side, across the litter of rocks and patches of bright green vegetation that formed the marge of the valley, and the valley itself, lush and full of stirrings. He heard a faint scraping behind and above him, and whirled, club lowered to chest height, muscles already tense. He looked.

It—*she*—was standing on a ledge to the side of the topmost rim of his cave entrance. He immediately recognized her as female, but female utterly unlike any he had ever seen. Her feet were long, her toes hooked firmly over the edge of the rock; her legs were also long, and smooth, and slim; and her breasts were round, high, wide-spaced, capped with pink nipples; and her face was a clear oval with a high forehead. She was hairless, except for the mane that framed her face and flowed down her broad shoulders. The mane was strangest of all. It changed as he watched, from deep ebony, to flame-red, to shimmering white.

He wanted her; she was not a tribeswoman, she was as different on the outside as he was inside . . . And with the wanting came an itch in his skull, an awareness—a consciousness. The consciousness flicked and danced, spreading from his head to his fingertips to the soles of his feet.

He scrambled toward the female; she skipped higher, and higher still, ascending the cliff effortlessly. Pebbles clattered as, digging nails and knees and elbows, scraping skin and panting, he gave chase. She reached the top of the cliff, a barren plateau devoid of soil and grass, devoid of anything save the gray stone that formed it, and she stood limned in the sun, the hair shimmering and changing. A dozen small pains tormented the surfaces of his body; his breath surged and moaned; his bones ached. Yet he fought his way toward her.

The sun's glare brightened, seemed to enfold the female, blinded him. When he could again see, she was gone.

Gone, too, was the consciousness. He was numb and plodding and would be for centuries—

(There are, I maybe ought to mention here, two kinds of human consciousness. One is the function of the cerebellum, evolution's idle whim. The other—? Well, that is what the savants have tried to explain, in vain. The wise men haven't even been able to *name* it, although they've tried: *the ideal forms, heaven, nirvana, the transcendent self, the vital principle, the Mystical Body* and *Man! Was I stoned,* to list a few silly attempts. These are, to the reality, as a bee-buzz is to a tuba concert. Those philosophers, they overcomplicate. The real thing is quite simple, as you'll learn shortly.)

—numb and plodding, he was, except for a few brief moments in each of his incarnations. It would be boring, and repetitious, to catalogue them all.

But—a random sampling:

He was tending his master's fence at the boundary marking estate grounds from the moor and she appeared, tall, slim, lovely, toes sunk in the marshy soil, hair changing from red to white. Instantly, he remembered, wanted. He vaulted the fence and chased her into the mists, onto the moor, skirting gulleys, leaping over quicksand pools. The shadows folded around her, and she was gone.

A hundred years later, he hauled his net from the brine,

paused to scan the rocky shore for his fellow fishermen, and saw her straddling the cleft between two boulders, toes fastened to the stone like pitons. Flinging the net aside, he ran, remembering, wanting. A spume of spray broke around her and for an instant she was haloed in glistening droplets, hair a rainbow, and as the halo disintegrated, she faded and was gone.

Gone, too, from the sand of Death Valley where he, a prospector, glimpsed her in the distant shimmer and, remembering, knew she wasn't a mirage. For a mirage would not have left ten perfect toe marks, miniature shafts, in the sand.

(This next anecdote will end the past and present parts of the story; we'll be getting to the future, prophetic and exciting part directly. Be patient, please. My telling of the incident will be rather detailed, because it happened relatively recently, ten years ago, and so I can recall it vividly.)

The sailor sat on a bench in a bus terminal in downtown Chicago, near the loop, staring at the cigarette-butt-littered floor, hearing, but not listening to, a tinny Christmas carol blaring from a jukebox.

> *God rest you merry, gentlemen,*
> *Let nothing you dismay . . .*

I'm dismayed, he thought. Who wouldn't be? Sitting in a strange city on the eve that people should be at home, the smell of pine and punch filling the nostrils, getting juiced with uncles, playing with nephews' toys, preparing for Midnight Mass, the special Mass one could attend juiced with no recriminations (Holy Mother the Church's great, unwritten dispensation.) The Savior is coming? Let Him. I won't be home. I am *en route* from nowhere—desk duty in the Holding Company barracks at the Naval Training Station, Great Lakes—to nowhere—desk duty aboard the *U.S.S. Lake Erie,* a twenty-five-year-old sub chaser with the highest non-reenlistment rate in either fleet. My sack of Christmas goodies is a seabag stuffed with dirty laundry, my gift a manila envelope containing mimeographed orders, in triplicate.

> *. . . to save us all from Satan's power*
> *When we had gone astray*

A little astray-going would be okay. I could enjoy going astray. But even if an ashtray chance should present itself, I couldn't take it, not with my bus for Providence—scenic, wonderful Providence, garden spot of the western world—leaving in less than thirty minutes, at 0300. How damn far astray can a guy go in half an hour? . . .

Abruptly, he realized he had been staring at bare feet planted firmly amidst the butts at the periphery of his vision. He glanced up briefly: a beautiful woman with odd hair, naked. He dropped his eyes, thinking the sight of a naked woman in a bus terminal at two-thirty on Christmas morning must be calculated to make him lose his cool, by someone—a huckster, probably—and this he refused to do, screw their game—

He remembered, wanted. And, of course, acted.

She glided down the up escalator as he bounded down the stairs, glided past the cigar counter to the revolving door as he charged with bent head, bull-fashion, in pursuit.

Shoes sliding on the icy sidewalk, blinded by whirls of snow and stung by wind, he slipped and stepped, and always she remained just beyond his grasp. He ignored the slush that bit his ankles. A sudden gust of air snatched his hat; he didn't care. He ran, she glided, and they reached the bank of the Lake, the strip of park behind the museum.

A blast of storm struck him directly, staggering him. He blinked and, yes, she was vanished, as he had known she would be. The water looked hard as metal, and empty.

In the final instants before his true consciousness dwindled and slept, he raged, he cried, "Damn you, bitch. I've been chasing you for forty thousand years and I'm *sick* of it. Either get in my life or get the *hell* out of it."

And, whispering, "I'm done with you."

He wasn't.

Why detail futility further? Nothing in the scenario changed much, except the setting and the body he happened to be wearing. He was short, tall, fat, thin, bald, hirsute, lusty, weak; she, always slim, rounded, magnificent. He was unsuccessful; she, elusive.

He was usually dying.

Men did a lot of dying in the century that followed—unpleasant deaths. The sins of the fathers were visited upon the sons. A million accumulated idiocies, an insane optimism, a perverse misuse of intelligence—these combined with the cauldron of poison the Earth had become to produce plagues, famines, cannibalism, unimaginable savagery. The infants whose mothers crushed their heads seconds after birth were the lucky ones.

(I'm not inserting a message; I'm not proselytizing. Merely telling a story. A love story. Even an optimistic love story. Have faith.)

To put it bluntly, Mankind survived. The race emerged from the holocaust free from folly and eventually attained its substitute, wisdom.

Slowly, carefully, humans rebuilt civilization—a civilization in harmony with the universe, instead of warring with it. So, when it came time to again leave the planet, man did not go in stink-and-fire belching machines, but on wings of shimmering energy drawn from the sources of creation, harnessed by the power of the mind. Man did not need cocoons of metal, for he went wrapped in the serene knowledge that he *belonged,* and this knowledge protected him from cold and heat and vacuum.

Men traveled everywhere, and learned much, and loved all they learned. (This is a love story.)

A billion suns burst into existence, aged, dwindled and died. A trillion planets gathered mass, gave birth to life, aged, dwindled, died.

Gradually, men discarded their physical forms—useless appendages, anachronisms—and spanned the parsecs as pure consciousness. And gradually, too, these consciousnesses aged, dwindled and died, for the race realized its continuance would serve no purpose. So it returned to nothingness, happy that it had been, content that it was no longer.

Before going, however, the race decreed that one of its number remain, to stand as a marker. He, the chosen, had been caveman, farmer, fisherman, sailor—oh, many things—and now he was the monument of his kind.

He existed. Time, with no one to note its passage, gave way to eternity, and still he existed, dozing in forever.

He awoke, and remembered, and remembering, was lonely. And he realized there was no *need* for loneliness. So he went to a place that was beginning anew, a place of suns and planets, and his mind touched atoms—formed, shaped, sculpted them into a remembered beauty, and gave the beauty awareness and womanhood, and called the woman Annie Mae. Then time began once more, the fruit of Annie Mae's sentience; time clutched the woman and, like a newly spun top, skidded and whirled, hurling her through the ages into the past, flinging her to a rocky hilltop, to a moor, and a seashore, and a Chicago bus station . . .

At last, time returned her to him. He moulded atoms around himself, clothing himself in a body, and greeted her.

She did not run.

He said, "I've been waiting for you."

They touched, kissed, embraced and there, at the beginning and the end, they made love.

That was the story.

After he finished the telling, they lay listening to the rain. Finally, the girl said, "I'm jealous."

"Why?"

"The woman you described, Annie Mae . . . she sounded like a Playboy centerfold or something. She didn't sound like *me.*"

"It was just a story."

"You believe it. Or you *want* to."

"Maybe."

She rolled to the edge of the bed and, looking at the wall, she said, "Danny, are we at the beginning or the end?"

"I don't know, angel. I honestly don't know."

But he did, and so did she.

FIREDAY: FIRENIGHT
Barry N. Malzberg

Here we all are in the Arena to watch the Day of Burning. Ricardo and Lucy and James and Leonard and Sophia and Dorothy and me. Many others as well, but this is my own unit; we go everywhere together under statute. The Arena is densely packed as it always is on these occasions; looking across the field toward the other end, we can see thousands and thousands, just like us, jammed against one another on the benches. Nevertheless, we are not uncomfortable, Ricardo and Lucy and James and Leonard and Sophia and Dorothy and me. We have worked out a seating arrangement. Only James is our problem.

Venders circulate, carrying souvenirs and refreshments, but we are not interested at this moment. We are involved in the Day of Burning, the earlier ceremonies of which have already begun. "Are you aware," Leonard says in his high, pedantic voice, "do you realize that hundreds of years ago men actually hoarded weapons and used these weapons purposefully in order to *kill* one another on the ground or from the air? Can you imagine a civilization such as that; what it must have been like for people to have lived and grown in that kind of world? Fortunately we have wiped all that from the human race, but now, every year, we celebrate the Day of Burning to remind us of how things were in those olden times and to be grateful that we are no longer savages. The Day of Burning shows us many interesting customs from those ancient lands." Leonard is that way. He says that he is going to be a teacher and seems to have an irresistible urge to explain things to us over and over again, but in this unit we understand one another and are grateful that Leonard is around to fill us in on interesting facts of history.

"True, all true, Leonard," Sophia says, who has a private relationship with him, "but we all know about the Day of Burning already, don't we?" She looks down the line of us, her little eyes glowing and serious and we nod; we do indeed all know about the Day of Burning. We are no longer youths but full apprentices, already deep into specialty training and the development of bonds in this unit that will last through our lives, and this is our fourth Day of Burning. As apprentices we have been permitted to come into the main Arena to watch the ceremonies from the beginning and are under only minimal supervision. Next year if all is well we will be under no instructions whatsoever.

"Look at this now," Dorothy says; "look at what they're doing." On the field, men who look like dwarfs from this distance are holding ancient pistols at one another and firing. Some of the men fall while others run, tossing the pistols in the air. They are all actors. All of the Day of Burning is pageant except for the very end of it. "Isn't that interesting? How terrible it must have been for those men! Isn't it wonderful that we don't live that way now!" Her round face flushes; she grasps my palm and runs her hands through the crevices, giving me a slow warmth. Dorothy will be my prime partner in the unit when we reach that stage, not that I will ignore the others or they Dorothy. Looking at her sideways, I apprehend as I have been more often in recent months, what it may be like, someday, to be more than an apprentice with her. "Don't you think?" she says, anxious for my approval, diminished by my silence, as is her way.

"Yes," I say, "it's terrible the way that they used to live, fighting wars and dropping death from the sky, but we don't live that way any more and the Day of Burning is a happy occasion, a happy time." Ricardo slaps me on the back, laughing out his agreement and a small bubble of tension which seemed to occur in the unit dissipates with a sigh. Now all the men with pistols leave the field for the next part of the ceremony and in the momentary lull the voices of the venders, their pacing through the stands come on insistently. "Do you want something?" I ask Dorothy.

"I don't know," she says. "Maybe yes. Maybe just a souvenir."

"A souvenir," says James, who will be my antagonist in the unit, "I would buy her nothing. She's selfish and spoiled. Also, souvenirs are not reckoned as necessary to the force of the pageant."

"Stop it, James," Dorothy says while the rest of us glare at him. In truth none of us get along with him very well; it is not his fault that he is the antagonist and eventually he will be assimilated into the unit as the last harmonious part, but that will only be in a few years when we have reached a level of sophistication which, perhaps, we do not yet possess. In the meantime, James as much as the rest of us suffers. "You have no right to say that and anyway, I want something."

"The souvenirs are didactic in intent, James," Leonard adds, leaning on his elbows to look down the line at James from where he is sitting. "They are meant to reinforce the message of the day, which is gratitude that we have moved beyond the stage of primitivism and are both healthy and recommended." Ricardo laughs at this—he is always laughing; he is the spirit of our unit—and hits James on the back much as he hit me, and Lucy motions for the vender to come over to our line. Looking at his tray, I find a miniature rifle which in the intensity of the sun reflects many colors and is curiously warm to the hand. "Would you like this?" I ask Dorothy.

"Yes," she says, "I will wear it as an ornament," and I take it from the vender's tray, give him the name and location of our unit and a fingertip identification and wave him away. Dorothy cups the rifle, turns it over, holds it against her dress. "It's pretty," she says. "It's terrible but it's pretty. I'll always remember this day." She presses my hand. "Thank you," she says and leans against me.

I put an arm around her. It would be pleasant if just once we could sit with one another in privacy without the remainder of the unit around us, but this is not to be, not for several years, and there is no point to pondering the impossible. Our rate of interaction, our manner of confluences are strictly charted according to procedure, and it is vital that the unit follow all the instructions as laid down by the proctors. Our level of attainment is controlled for our benefit. Our lives are controlled, so is the progress of our relationships, because only in that way will the unit mature properly. All of this was worked out a long time ago by the technicians, resolved that the history re-enacted in the Day of Burning never come to pass again. We have shed the violence and idiocy of the old times; we celebrate our new mode of living. Nevertheless, I would like to be alone with Dorothy.

"Now," Leonard says, "we're going to move into the more social areas, the more widespread and generalized killing." He points toward the sky in which, over the past few moments while I have been absorbed, antique airplanes have been massing ominously, droning out their danger like a snore. On the field itself, thousands of actors in costume spill from the side doors and run out frantically to mill around, shouting at one another. "They're going to simulate a bombing now," Leonard whispers, pedanticism drained from his voice by excitement. "Watch this now."

In every one of the units gathered in the stands there is one like Leonard to explain and discuss the events of the Day of Burning. This is how the units were prepared, and we are lucky to have him. Nevertheless, I have a spell of irritation; it really would be much better and more interesting if the Day of Burning had a master of ceremonies and—as I understand was the case before the units became organized and cohesive—a set of loud-speakers so that all of the events could be explained before and as they happen. This would be far more appealing and dramatic. My only objection to the Day of Burning which otherwise I enjoy is that it is entirely too matter-of-fact and that if Leonard were not around to explain things or if Leonard were to have a lapse, we would miss much of the significance. As it is, of course, we miss nothing and I regret my anger at Leonard, no matter how momentary. The Day of Burning is a good thing, a wonderful thing, and shows us how far we have gone in shedding the dreadful customs of our forebears. It is interesting and fascinating as well as being highly educational and I am sorry that even for an instant I have questioned the manner of its presentation. Dorothy must sense what I am thinking without being able to understand it and looks up at me. "Don't," she says, "don't worry. We don't live that way any more."

"I know," I say, "it hasn't been this way for hundreds of years."

"And we'll never live that way again. We live in units now, which is the way we should have always lived, and with the units nothing bad can ever happen to us again. There will never be another burning." She is not the brightest of our unit, but possibly the most sensitive. I feel a spell of sentiment for her and do not relinquish my hold. Ricardo taps me yet again on the back. "Don't daydream," he says, squeezing Lucy's hand. "You two should pay attention," and then he laughs. Ricardo gives the laughter to the unit.

"Yes," James says, spiteful and antagonistic as he must be, "that's very easy for all of you to say, but how do you know what you're watching? What do you think this all means? How do you know that the burning is behind? They can lie to us, they can lie to everyone and no one would know the difference. It's all a mockery." As the antagonist of the unit, James is the only one who has not been sex-paired, and this I believe makes him bitter; in any event I can understand his happiness as the seventh member, the only one doomed to be without a partner. "You're all fools," James says angrily; "you're like ants in a colony, you fools and your precious unit, always talking about the unit and the mentors and the advisers as if it were the whole world, when sometime, anytime at all, a heel could come down and crush us out of existence. It may be doing it now, for all we know. It may be about to happen this second while we sit and watch this stupid Day of Burning." James is an extremely unhappy and antagonistic individual, but his role has been defined by genetics and socio-dynamics no less than Ricardo's, and I bear him no ill feeling. Ricardo brings the laughter, Leonard the pedagogy, Dorothy the tenderness, James the doubt. All of them parts of the construct, all of them integral to the whole. I cancel down my feelings of hostility (years ago I hated James, but now as I move near the end of the apprentice stage I feel sympathy for him) and, shaking my head, concentrate on the events in the Arena.

The planes are pouring down death from the sky. Looking

up at them through the sudden haze and pall against the landscape, I can see the ozone, taste the smoke, inhale the flames. Now I know again why it is truly called the Day of Burning. On the field the actors continue to mill, more and more agitatedly, some of them now falling in place, their curiously colored costumes stains against the earth. "They're beginning to be overcome now," Leonard says judiciously. "Soon all of them will be dead. This is the way it used to be, you know. Whole villages and cities were destroyed from the air. It is a time of gratitude now that we have gone beyond this darkness."

Dorothy shudders against me. I hold her more closely. Lucy inhales sharply, a small whimper of horror coming from her, and I can hear Ricardo talking rapidly to her in a low voice, comforting her; can see Leonard talking to Sophia intensely as well now that the actors are falling over on the field by the hundreds, toppling like marionettes to roll and at last lie still on the earth and still the planes lance down their fire. The noise is terrific; increasing and overcoming all of our conversation for instants, the stands of the Arena shaking, clattering underneath us, the benches seeming to inflate beneath us so that balance is threatened and still the remorseless planes pound away. All of the actors are down now except for a few forms staggering through the haze. The haze closes in completely on the terrain and those actors, too, fall. The haze covers everything. The planes build to an increase of sound and then depart. They mass high above us in a crucifix and then are gone, speeding toward the sea where, as we know from the litany of the Day of Burning, they will perish in the waves, all of them being manned by robots programmed to self-destruct after the ceremony.

"Wasn't that interesting?" Leonard says. The actors are still down. "That's the way it actually used to be with the ancients. Of course we are no longer that way at all and are grateful that we have the yearly Day of Burning to remind us, if reminding need be, what we used to be and what we have become. Villages, even whole cities, but now actors—"

"How do you know they're actors?" James says angrily, standing in place, shouting, as machinery moves in from the sides of the Arena to shovel up the actors and in carting devices take them away and underneath. "All of us are always saying they're actors, saying that the planes are robots, saying that the Day of Burning is a ceremony, but how do we *know*—" He stops, babbling, suffused with rage. Around us, other units look at James curiously, some faces with anger. It is not customary to stand in the audience in the Arena on the Day of Burning, which is a time of witness and recollection, not activity. James has broken that code. "Sit," voices cry, "you're blocking the way. We can't see, be quiet, sit!" and so on, but James stands against this, his mouth still moving, trying to talk. No one, however, can hear him, because of the angry voices. Finally it is Ricardo who leaps to his feet and drags James into place, James fighting him all the way until Ricardo applies a special hold and then James collapses in place, his face pale. "A lie," he says, "it's all a lie. You'll see. You'll learn."

"Come on, James, don't ruin the day," Ricardo says in his jocular way, laughing again, slamming James on the back, but James does not respond. His face becomes more painful, his voice, dropping in level, ominous. "You'll see," he says, "you'll see what the Day of Burning means, you and everybody else in this accursed unit. I curse all of you. I curse the mentors. I curse the unit and the day I was created to be its antagonist. I curse the Day of Burning."

"It is necessary," Leonard says, leaning over Sophia to address the rest of us, still holding her hand, "necessary in every unit that a microcosm of the old society exist; the antagonist must be present as well so that we can see and gaze upon and know those forces which afflicted the ancients, and the role of the antagonist is vital. But as we become older and more integrated, there will be less tension and you, too, James will become one of us. Now, let us watch the rest of the ceremonies," he says dismissively and turns back toward the field where the next actors are coming out, a small group who are to depict heads of state tossing insults and threats at one another.

"Lies," James says quietly, shaking his head, hands folded, looking at the concrete beneath us. "It's all lies. You'll see. You'll learn." He closes his eyes. He quiets.

"I'm afraid of him," Dorothy says. "I'm afraid of him. Tell me not to be afraid, but I am afraid; someday he's going to do something terrible. Something terrible to all of us; I know it." She has never said this before. I hold her and mumble comfort. There is nothing else to do.

I look at the sky, which is clear again. The planes are gone. With James silent, the unit is together again. Ricardo laughs and hits me on the back. I feel pain.

LOSTLING
John Brunner

"Package for you," said a half-seen figure from the doorstep. The voice was harsh and flat, more than somewhat like a poor telephone connection.

"What?" Bleary-eyed with sleep, shivering in his pajamas, Ted Kingsley was on the verge of fury. "At three o'clock in the morning? You must be crazy!"

"Ha-ha," the figure said with no trace of amusement. "You are Theodore William Kingsley, aren't you?"

"Uh—yes!"

"Well, that's the name on the label." A large parcel was thrust into Ted's arms. "Though to my way of ratiocinating the deal is crazy, like you said. I mean, letting one of these be delivered in a run-down neighborhood like yours—!"

"Now just a second!" Having taken a grip on the package more by reflex than intention, Ted bridled. He was very proud of the fact that he and Molly lived in this district. It was the absolute opposite of run-down: a development of brand-new houses that cost a mint of money.

But the stranger had disappeared.

"What in the world is going on?" Molly demanded, belting the sash of her robe around her as she hurried down the stairs, barefooted. "What's that you've got there?"

Pushing shut the front door, Ted said rather foolishly,

"It's a parcel." It was heavy; he set it down on the hall table next to the phone directories.

"Who's it from?" Obviously Molly wasn't fully awake either.

"Some idiot who has things delivered in the small hours!" Ted's eyes were finally regaining their normal focus. He was able to read the label now.

"It's addressed to us okay," he said. "Mr. and Mrs. Theodore William Kingsley. And it's from the Betastok Reproduction Company."

"Betastok? Where's that? Somewhere in Russia, isn't it?"

"Very funny," Ted growled. "No! It says here it's at Underlevel Five, Bering City X2 X4 X8. Hell, it must be a practical joke. Let's go back to bed."

"An expensive joke, then!" Molly said. "That label's in some sort of luminous ink. Haven't you noticed?"

"I thought it was just my eyesight," Ted muttered sourly.

"Reproduction Company," Molly mused, inspecting the package for herself. "Could it be something to do with your job?" Ted worked as assistant technical manager of a printing firm. "A sales promotion gimmick? Isn't 'stock' something to do with grades of paper?"

"If anybody thinks he's going to promote a deal with me by having samples delivered at this ungodly hour—!"

"Oh, let's open it," Molly said, lifting the parcel and pushing aside the living-room door with her toes. "I'm too wide-awake to go straight back to bed, anyhow."

"Oh, my Lord!" Ted sighed, but followed her.

She had set the parcel down on their big coffee table and was turning it around, examining it. It was about two feet long by two wide, and a foot deep, and its whole exterior was a smooth light blue, with no sign of string or tape.

"I don't see how to open it," she confessed. "Can you hand me the paperknife from the bureau?"

Resignedly Ted obliged, and after much effort she managed to tear the top of the wrapping and peel it back.

"There's a note inside," she announced, pulling out a sheet of bright blue paper with writing on it. " 'Dear and much-valued client'—it says—'we are certain that you will be delighted with the quality of our product, so superior to the version produced by unskilled labor. Provided you follow the instructions exactly, your purchase will give you a lifetime of pleasure and satisfaction, and you will be the envy of your less fortunate acquaintances. . . .' Tiddly-pom and et cetera." She tossed the letter aside and dug deeper into the package.

"Instruction manual!" she reported triumphantly, and threw at Ted a blue booklet with bold pink lettering on the cover. He caught it automatically. "And—hmm . . .!"

She removed in rapid succession a flat box labeled MAINTENANCE KIT I, a long cylinder labeled FUEL, and another box, rather larger, labeled MAINTENANCE KIT II (FOR EMERGENCY USE ONLY), and also a considerable amount of packing material, a curious fluffy substance resembling orange kapok.

Ted gathered these into a neat pile, wishing to goodness he were comfortably back in bed, and waited for her to delve to the bottom of the parcel.

Tossing aside the last of the packing, she exposed a rigid container with a transparent lid—and stopped dead in midmotion.

"What is it?" Ted demanded, too weary to move closer and look for himself. "Some pointless bit of gadgetry or other?"

"Ted!" Molly's voice broke. "It's—it's a baby!"

"You must mean a doll," Ted said eventually.

"*Doll?* Smiling up at me and waving its arms and legs?"

Frantically, Molly was trying to lift the lid of the container. "Oh, what crazy sadist could have done this?"

In response to accidental pressure on an unseen catch, the lid flew aside. She reached down and produced—yes, a baby! A naked boy, probably a few weeks old, with big blue eyes and a sparse thatch of blond hair. She cuddled him close and began to croon reassuringly, "There, there! There, there— Ted, don't just stand around like an idiot! It's cold in here! Light the gas fire! Find a blanket for him, or something!"

Dazed, Ted complied; then, with a sudden access of inspiration, he dived for the "maintenance manual" he had let fall. He leafed rapidly through it.

"Oh, my Lord!" he said in a thin voice. "It *is* an instruction book for a baby! Look, anatomical drawings!"

"But . . .!" Molly turned pale.

"Listen, will you? It says on the first page, 'Congratulations on being allotted a Betastok A-Star limited-edition infant with a fully comprehensive guarantee! In case you are in any doubt, your new acquisition is'—and then it says in different print on a dotted line, 'male.' And it goes on, 'It will respond to being called'—and then there's a name added on another dotted line. 'Felix'!"

The baby looked up perkily and gave a nod. Then, unexpectedly, he turned his head and seemed to survey the room. Instantly his former grin was displaced by a scowl, and he started to wail at the top of his lungs.

"The poor darling must be hungry!" Molly exclaimed. "Go warm some milk, and I'll see if I can feed him with a spoon!"

"Wait!" Ted was still frenziedly ruffling pages. "This is incredible! It says here under 'Sonic Evidence of Malfunction' that low-degree varishability and disproportionate biasing of the thaumatroper may sometimes result in unsystematized vo-calization, or as it is colloquially known, 'screaming'!"

"What?" Molly shouted over the continued squalling of Felix.

"It's all like that!" Ted insisted. "Gibberish! Double talk! Here's another bit. 'Apparently Delayed Response to Data-Input. It is within the normal range of variation of such a complex product as our A-Star line for response not to be evoked immediately when the above introjections are per-formed. Do not worry. By the nine-week mark at latest, cal-culus, topology, Cantorian transfinites and n-dimensional ma-trix modulation will all be firmly implanted in the cortex. See guarantee.' "

"Oh, don't waste any more time on that rubbish!" Molly snapped, still vainly trying to soothe Felix into silence. "Go to the kitchen, will you? Hurry!"

"I'm more inclined to ring the police," Ted said grimly, and turned to the door, tossing the instruction manual on the coffee table.

"Stop!"

The order, in a thin, high, ill-tempered tone, froze him in his tracks. Molly cried out.

"He—*he* said that! The baby spoke!"

"Yes, of course I did!" Felix rasped. With puny fists he forced himself into an upright position against Molly's bosom. "I don't know what those idiots at the company think they're playing at, sending me to a couple of yuggish morons in a slum like this! I'm going to file a complaint and sue them for every centicredit they possess! Where's your varisher, and why aren't I in it? What do you imagine you're supposed to do with a baby when you unpack it—leave it exposed to the open air?"

There was a dead, horrible pause. Eventually Ted swallowed a huge though nonexistent lump in his throat and said, "I—I don't think we own a varisher."

"No varisher?" Felix turned almost purple. "I'm likely to be traumatized for life at this rate! I don't believe it! Next you'll be telling me you haven't bought a thaumatroper, either!"

Ted dumbly shook his head.

"But this is abominable!" Felix was jerking around with such violence now, he was almost slipping out of Molly's arms. "My contract said I was going to a decent family—nothing very fancy, just a middle-bracket executive home, sub-lux but sound and with good prospects of parental advancement soon. . . . And where do I wind up? In this squalid, disgusting, insanitary, dangerous *hovel!* I didn't know places like this existed any more!"

Ted stared at him in total, utter and unqualified bewilderment. He was barely even able to think how absurd it was to be talking to a baby who could be no more than a month old.

Seizing on the one word in the previous tirade which seemed to make sense, Molly said, "Dangerous? But there's nothing to be afraid of here!"

Felix pointed a tiny finger at the gas fire. "You think combustion isn't dangerous? Don't make me laugh! The whole damned house could oxidize in a flash, if this room is a fair sample—wooden floor, wooden table, fabric draperies! And what about my not being properly varished, hm? That's definitely dangerous! I'm having to use cortical channels that aren't due to be exploited for at least another week, simply to protect my own existence! Get your hands back on that manual and look up the final section, 'Emergency Procedure'—and don't try and make out that this isn't an emergency, because I'm telling you it is!"

"You'd better do as he says," Molly whispered.

Fingers all thumbs, Ted obeyed. At the back of the booklet —which, he suddenly realized, was ridiculously thin compared to say a volume of Spock—he did indeed find a section headed "Emergency Procedure." He read aloud from it at random.

" 'Temperature in Excess of Optimum. Administer one drop of contents of Phial Y from Maintenance Kit I. Discoloration of Epidermis, i.e., Readings G or H on comparison chart—' "

"Not that part!" Felix howled. "The next bit, where it tells you how to couple Maintenance Kit II to the plasma supply!"

"Plasma?" Ted echoed. "You have to have a blood transfusion, is that it?"

"Imbecile!" Felix was flailing around with both arms and both legs, and his voice was an ear-piercing, nape-prickling yell. "*Plasma!* Gas at stellar temperature! You mean you don't even have mains power?"

"Of course!" Molly burst out. She waved a shaking hand at the electric lamps. But Ted checked her. A sudden dazzling inspiration had invaded his mind.

"I don't think that's what he's talking about," he said slowly. "Felix, where did you expect to be delivered?"

"Threeple-nine-wow totter-oot-hah Upper Runcible Pavement, where else?" Felix snapped. Abruptly a great light seemed to dawn on him, too. "You mean this isn't the right place?"

"I'm not even sure it's the right time," Ted said, and had to draw extra breath. He glanced around and spotted the letter which Molly had first extracted from the parcel. He seized it, looking for a date. He found one. He said faintly, "This letter seems to have been written on—"

"February 30th, 2361," a voice interrupted.

"Who said that?" Ted cried, and Molly, gasping, nearly let

Felix fall to the floor.

"I did," the same voice answered, and—and *someone* was in the room with them. At first there was only a vague-edged cloud; then, a second later, there was a small man with a sallow skin, his expression extremely worried, wearing a peculiar one-piece garment which sometimes looked green and sometimes yellow, carrying a thing that hurt Ted's eyes when he tried to look directly at it.

"My apologies," this intruder said in a harassed tone. "We had some irrelevant extrapinkling on the dispatch nodes of our multiwarper, and— But never mind that! At least I've managed to locate the misdirected goods."

He brightened visibly and favored first Molly, then Ted, with a broad grin. It wasn't a very pleasant grin. His teeth were of at least four different colors, and one of them was a shade they'd neither seen before nor even dreamed of.

"Allow me!" he went on, and reached for Felix, who had begun to howl again. But the howling stopped the moment the stranger touched him.

"There!" the latter said, sounding pleased, and dropped the baby back into the box he had arrived in. "Thank goodness he was insured—after a calamity like this, he wouldn't be any good to anyone, of course. Well, I needn't trouble you any longer. Come to think of it, though . . ." He hesitated. "I must say it was very astute of you, considering your primitive level of civilization, to work out so rapidly what must have happened. My compliments. Your four-times-great-grandson certainly does have the sort of heredity which justifies taking on a Betastok A-Star model infant!"

"Our—what?" Ted whispered. Molly came to stand close against him, trembling.

"Oh, that's how the confusion arose. Same name—same

somatic type—an exceptionally high correspondence rate on the phrenotracker—and the temporal-coefficient notator slipped a notch. It does happen now and then, as it were. Well, sorry you've been bothered. Good morning, or afternoon, or whatever it is in your particular zone."

"Wait!" Molly cried. The stranger was blurring at the edges. "What have you done to Felix?"

"Switched him off, of course. I mean, *you* couldn't cope with him, and after this traumatization the original client wouldn't want him, would he? I'm sorry I can't take him back with me, incidentally, but the tariff on inanimate organics is prohibitive. Still, the protein will be a slight compensation for your trouble. It's best to roast it with a little garlic."

"Are you mad?" Ted exploded, and felt Molly sway beside him. "You may think we're primitive, but we're not cannibals!"

"Of course not!" the stranger said, looking shocked. "He may appear human, he may be indistinguishable from the human except mentally—but he isn't. I ought to know! After all, I issue three hundred like him every week. . . . Oh, I guess I shouldn't have said that. I'll be on my way before I let slip anything else compromising. Good-by!"

And he wasn't there.

"Ted," Molly said, when at last she had stopped her teeth from chattering, "how can we explain a dead baby?"

"But it wasn't a baby," Ted muttered. "You heard the man."

"I know. But who's going to believe us?"

She was right. Nobody did.

THE AMBIGUITIES OF YESTERDAY
Gordon Eklund

Click.

In the deep silence of the swamp the sound of the camera's snapping shutter seemed as loud and certain as a gunshot. *Click.* Holding his breath, Alfred ducked down, regaining his nook behind the bare scrub bush which concealed him from the men. He listened but they had not heard; they were talking again.

"No need to kill them," said one, his words drawled slowly —painfully—so that Alfred could barely decipher their intended meaning. "Only hurt them—you know—scare them off."

"That's as bad as killing them," said another. "Except then they can talk. And you know these boys will."

"Sure," said a third. "They come here. Who invited them? Me? You? The sheriff or mayor? Are we going to let this one fellow go running home free as a crow to New York so he can tell all his blonde girlie friends how he outsmarted all us rednecks? We took them. Now we have to kill them."

"You bet," said the big man—who wore a tan uniform and a wide hat—the sheriff. He laughed. "Down in this swamp. Hell, who's ever going to find them here?"

"Who'll ever look?" asked the first man.

Alfred stood clutching the miniature camera tightly in his

dry palm. *Click. Click.* In the harsh illumination of the automobile headlights, he was unable to discern the particular features of any of these men. They were faceless beings. He saw only their figures—vague, misty shapes of humanity. Three were handcuffed. These were not talking. *Click.* He crouched down, the dank mud sucking at his bootheels.

"Then it's decided," said the sheriff. "We have to shoot the three of them." Turning lightly on a heel, he faced the handcuffed men. "Sorry, boys," he said.

Alfred gripped his stomach, peering easily through the gaps in the scrub bush. These years had a certain smell to them. The odor came clearly now, a stink transcending the literal rot of the swamp. The 1960's carried the odor of a recently dead beast. The animal was just now stiffening, only faintly beginning to stink. In ten years' time, the odor was much worse. By 1980, it was nearly unbearable. In 1990, it was awesomely foul. Alfred had been born in 1997; he was forty-two years old. In his own time of 2039, the odor was so intense no one recognized it any more; the odor was part of the air.

The sheriff arranged the three handcuffed men in a rigid line. As if in expectation, the automobile headlights dimmed. A pair of flashlights beamed instead, flickering from face to face. Alfred jumped up. *Click. Click.*

"Turn around."

"You're afraid to face us."

"I said turn."

Click.

Alfred observed through the spyhole of his camera. Inside a pocket of deep blackness, a red fire flashed. There was a reverberation which shook the overhanging trees. *Click.* The gun fell temporarily silent as it was passed from hand to hand. A man fell on his face. Another suddenly wept. Red fire. A shot.

Bang. Click. Bang. Two men fell together.

"Christ," said a man.

Click.

"Here—look here." A flashlight trailed through the mud. *Click.* "They bleed the same as us." He was laughing. "How about that?"

Alfred clicked his camera hastily, seeking the end. He had smelled enough of this time. The foulness clutched at his gut, bending him double. Done, he shoved the camera deep in a pocket. Ahead, the men were moving, dragging the limp bodies of the dead toward the deep dark recesses of the swamp. Their voices, as they worked, came in shrill excited whispers. Alfred shut his eyes. The swamp disappeared. In his mind, Alfred saw pictures of another world. Here was a torn, ravaged city of rubble and ruin. He picked his way down a broken street and came upon a single white house standing amid the refuse. He mounted the front stairs, entered the house, and passed a room in which a child soundly slept. In a second room, the walls lined with old books, bindings torn and stained, he focused upon a single chair, seeing it well, the wrinkled fabric, a puddle of spilled coffee. His lips moved silently, as if in prayer.

When he opened his eyes, he was sitting in the chair in the room among the old books. The gentle noises of the slumbering child reached him plainly. His hands trembled. Grasping his stomach, he stood, doubled over, and sprang for a window.

He was home again.

"This is all?" cried the professor. He slammed his fist down upon the flat surface of the table. "A dozen photographs. All useless. What did you do, Alfred?" His fist struck again—savagely. "Did you fall asleep in that swamp? Were you overcome by fatigue? Am I working you too hard, poor man?"

"No," Arthur said quickly. "Of course not. I—I'm sorry." Although Alfred stood, it was the tiny hunched figure of the professor seated in a chair who dominated the room. "I tried. But what if they'd heard me—seen me? What then?"

"In that event, using your talent, you would have escaped." The professor was gazing at the photographs again, bringing them up close to his face and staring intently. He rubbed his eyes, raised his head, glared. "A thousand times I have told you, Alfred. I do not want photographs of men who are dead. I want to see the faces—the eyes—of the living. What you bring me is useless. My book . . ." Breaking off, he sighed, leaning back in the chair. He lifted his eyes to the cracked crumbling ceiling of his study. "I will pay you nothing."

"But you must."

"For this—" indicating the photographs—"no."

"Then I won't do it again," Alfred said bravely.

"You will starve. The gangs will eat you."

"No. I'll—" Already, Alfred sensed the ebbing of his courage. "I'll leave the city. I'll farm. I'll—"

"Your son will die first. I am a wealthy man, Alfred. You must do as I say."

"Yes. But pay me. Please. We have nothing."

"Tomorrow," the professor said. "In the morning you will undertake another assignment. If you return bearing the proper photographs, then"—he stood, approaching Alfred, hurling a sudden slender arm around his shoulders, drawing him toward a cluttered corner of the room—"I will pay you double."

"In food?"

"Yes. Water. Anything. Will you do it?"

Alfred said, "Yes."

Smiling, the professor released Alfred and reached into a desk drawer. He withdrew a thick sheaf of papers covered with jerky penciled notes. Carefully, as though he alone comprehended the pattern present amid apparent chaos, he turned the pages. "Here," he said at last, holding out a paper. Alfred accepted the page. "Here is what I need. It will please Father Gordon's persecution complex as well."

Alfred attempted to decipher the jumbled phrases. One word—a name—stood out clearly. "But I've already seen this," he said.

"No," the professor said. "That was the first brother. The President. There were two who were shot. Both Catholics, fortunately. This one occurred in 1968. In California. Before you leave, I will provide you the necessary details and a photograph of the actual scene."

"Why always this?" Alfred demanded angrily. "Death and murder, riot and slaughter?" He spoke largely to himself—for himself. "Before I met you, I saw happiness, laughter, children, mothers. Before you—"

"You idiot." The professor smoked, filling the cloistered air with clouds of dreary gray. "My book does not have room for stupid laughing children. I seek the visage of Satan himself. You should feel blessed to participate in such a divine quest. Why do you think God granted you your holy talent?"

"That was my father. And he wasn't God." Alfred giggled. "Maybe he was Satan."

The professor smiled grimly. "Satan we shall find here," he said, slapping the pages of his notes. "But with your help, Alfred. Only with your help."

Alfred nodded. The professor had hired him a year ago, when starvation loomed very near. For the first time, his inherited ability to visit the past had been turned toward a serious end. The professor's book—a history—would be the first such volume in twenty years, the definitive account of the Years of

Madness between 1960 and 1990. Alfred performed research. The professor had a theory.

"You know my theory," he told Alfred, regaining his seat. "But until I have gathered sufficient first-hand evidence, I dare not begin the actual composition of my book. Father Gordon demands it. My pride does likewise. Satan!" he cried, gesturing at the far wall, where a painting of Christ upon the cross stood tacked between two great gaping holes in the plaster. The colors were cool and subdued, except for the hands and feet, where pools of crimson blood burned like the light of a dying sun. "Who else could have caused the downfall of the human race in so few years? Yet Father Gordon insists the causes may be natural and demands proof before sanctifying my work. My colleagues cry paranoia, but I shall prove them fools, ostrichs, heads buried in the sands of timidity. When published, my book will send the world rushing to my side. Together, we shall drive Satan back to his lair."

"What world?" Alfred asked. He gazed through a dirty window, seeing below the infrequent scattered fires of the city. He knew what lay out there: the dying, starving, the dead or desperate beasts who had once been free men but who now merely continued to exist in the shattered remains of this great city built by ancestors who—compared to them—were as gods. And Alfred alone, through his talent, was able to visit those years when gods had truly walked the earth. And why? What was he permitted to see? Only the killing, destruction, madness. He turned suddenly upon the professor with a look of utter disgust.

But he said nothing. The professor was staring at a photograph. "Here," he said, not looking up. "I can almost make him out. Come here and tell me about this man."

A cold shiver crossed Alfred's soul. He approached cautiously. Peering past the professor's tiny shoulders, he saw the swamp, a cluster of men surrounding three fallen bodies. The professor tapped one figure, a face hidden in deep shadow. "Who is this?"

"I don't have any idea."

"You lie. Why have you no clear photograph of him?"

"I couldn't. He was just a man. There were a dozen there."

"You idiot. That's him."

"Who?" cried Alfred, turning his back. "You don't know what you're talking about," he whispered.

"That," the professor said, "is him. The devil." He slapped the table. "Don't you think I'd know him anywhere?"

The windows in the room were tightly sealed at night to prevent the intrusion of unnecessary dust and filth. In spite of this, the howling reached Alfred clearly. The voice was high-pitched, filled with pain and terror. Alfred knew it meant the gang had caught another mutant, one drawn from its hiding place in search of food or water. Now the gang was killing the mutant in the usual fashion—slowly, through torture, relentlessly, without mercy. And when they were done, they would feast. And why not? Was a mutant a human being? Was a man the same as an ape? Was it cannibalism to consume the flesh of such a creature? Or was it no different from eating the meat of a cow, chicken, fish?

Standing, Alfred went to the window and used a balled fist to clear a hole through the caked dust upon the glass. Across the street—in the broken wreck of a brick building—a fire burned. The screams came from there—but fitfully now. At the edge of the horizon, the first faint rays of the dawning sun licked vaguely at the black sky. But Alfred didn't want to see. He wished the mutant dead, gone, silent. He didn't want the screams to wake his son.

He went back to where he had been sitting and, standing above the small table, gazed down upon the photographs neatly arranged in a circle. In each the scene was radically different. Seeing them now brought back the actual moment as plainly as if it were today. Here was the Nazi death camp in Poland—the spiritual beginning of the Years of Madness. The streets of Dallas, Texas, and the pale assassin of John Kennedy. The nuclear device smuggled anonymously into New York Harbor to initiate the Last War. The riots in Watts, Detroit, San Francisco, and Calcutta. The massacre at Songmy. Each photograph, though different in time and place, was also similar, for death is rarely a singular event; dead men share the same gaze, expression, emotions.

And the living? They, too, were different—except for the one man, the one face.

Sitting, Alfred shifted his gaze from scene to scene, each time meeting that same face. The man was not old. Neither was he young. Ageless. His flesh as pale as the fallen snow Alfred remembered from childhood. Blond hair. A recessed brow and jutting jaw. A slender man dressed in the garments of his time: an SS uniform; the American army; a policeman. But the face was always the same.

Who was he?

Alfred asked this question, not expecting an answer, as he had asked it each waking moment since he had first noticed this one face which he met everywhere. Was this truly the face of Satan? The long red scar curling from forehead to jaw was evidence of some humanity. But it was all.

Why had he kept these photographs secret? Alfred asked this question, too. Here among the photographs he had snapped today were two that clearly showed that same slender figure and pale scarred face. This man was the one the professor had somehow recognized—even in shadowed profile—as someone exceptional, as the devil. Alfred feared the professor, once shown such firm evidence to support his theory, would discontinue his research, depriving Alfred of his immediate livelihood. Then he would die. And Thomas, too. So he kept the existence of these photographs secret as a matter of sheer survival.

Or was that only a transparent lie he no longer believed himself? Once apprised of the truth, wouldn't the professor demand more evidence, not less?

Wasn't the truth instead that this man—or devil—was too familiar. Alfred thought he knew him. The features were clear, distinct: this man was someone he had known.

But where? When?

"Father?"

"Oh." Hastily, Alfred gathered the photographs and thrust them inside his shirt. Then he turned, smiling at his son. Thomas was twelve, bright, blond, healthy. He had the talent, but he was normal.

"Weren't those pictures?"

"Yes," Alfred said.

"Like the others?" Thomas waved at the walls of the room, which were decorated with a multitude of reproductions of his own face and form, a display of growth and development from birth until now. "I want to see them." Alfred not only loved his son, he worshiped him. How else could a father react in these times when gifted with a perfect son?

"No," Alfred said. "These pictures are the ones I take for the professor. When I go back."

"Let me see them." The boy held out his hand.

Alfred crossed the room quickly. "I can't."

"Why? You're not afraid of me, are you?"

"Why should I be? You're my son."

"But my talent is stronger than yours."

"That's not it," Alfred said, though it was true. So far, Thomas had made only a few, ostensibly brief journeys into the past; he still required Alfred's help and guidance. But his talent was strong—stronger than Alfred's, as his in turn had exceeded his own father's. Alfred could remain in the past for no more than an hour. Already—on one occasion—refusing to return—laughing while Alfred pleaded—Thomas had spent a full day in 1909. "And I could have stayed longer," he had said, upon returning. "But it was boring back there."

Thomas approached his father. "Let me come with you this time." He still held his hand—steady and deliberate—in front of him. A smile touched his lips. "I know you're going."

From without came a scream.

"Another one?" Thomas said, dropping his hand.

"A mutant," said Alfred.

"Ah, food," said Thomas. He wiped his lips with his tongue, then grinned. "Dinner."

"Stop that. We're mutants, too. You and I. If they caught you, they'd kill you."

"They'd never know."

"They would." Alfred had once been cornered by the gang. Only by leaping into the past had he avoided his own death. "I don't know how. They can see it in our eyes—smell it—the strangeness."

"Oh, you're crazy. We're not monsters. We're men. Better than men."

"No, we're the same. We have a talent, but we're human. We're men."

"You are," Thomas said. He extended himself full-length, stretching and yawning. "I should sleep more." He turned, gazing out the window, where the faint light of early morning trickled across the ruined landscape. "I can see their fire burning. I think they killed it."

"I can smell it," Alfred said.

"I'm still going with you," Thomas said.

"No, you're not."

"Then I'll have to make you." The boy approached his father on tiptoes. Alfred gazed down at his feet, seeing nothing there. Suddenly, throwing back an arm, Thomas struck. Alfred whimpered, nearly falling under the blow. Thomas hit him again—flat across the mouth. Alfred tasted blood on his lips.

"Well?" asked the boy.

"No," Alfred whispered, tears in his eyes. He would not —could not.

"You're asking for it." Thomas balled his fist and hit again. Alfred cried out and fell to his knees. He tried to stand but Thomas, raising a foot, kicked him in the chest.

"You old fool," said the boy.

After finally getting Thomas to bed, Alfred returned to the study and sat down. Through the dust-choked window behind, the light of early morning battled to gain entrance. He ought to be leaving now; the professor expected him back before noon. His camera lay in readiness. But he knew he was afraid. The odor of charred flesh permeated the air. His face—cut and scratched—hurt him. Already in the past few hours he had seen too much killing and death. In Mississippi, three innocent men had died. One here—a mutant. And now he would have to witness yet another killing.

He stared at the photograph the professor had given him, struggling to concentrate, trying to study the design and pattern of this snapshot of yesterday. The photograph revealed a large, plush hotel ballroom. Alfred continued to stare at the photograph until he could see it with his eyes shut. He sighed, knowing he was ready. Parting the curtain of time with an ease born of practice, he slipped backward. Throughout history men had speculated upon ways and means of traveling freely into the past. Time machines had been imaginatively constructed, marvelous gadgets, quite unnecessary. Time flowed in a single constant direction, but any man—given the proper awareness—could reverse this flow and proceed backward. Alfred's forefathers had been granted this awareness through fateful evolution and the talent had passed easily through their blood. His earliest ancestors, unable to control their abilities, had been damned as madmen and locked away in asylums. Later generations had learned to keep their talent secret. In time, Alfred's father had developed his talent to the point where he could deliberately dart backward for long moments at a time, selecting his time and location in advance. Alfred could remain in the past a full hour. And Thomas even longer.

Alfred was moving now, but he would not look. Once, when very young, he had, opening his eyes upon a horrible churning tunnel of utter blackness. He had nearly been lost; only his father had saved him. Now the years flowed invisibly past. His stomach twisted and fluttered. The forty-two years of his own life passed in a flash, for those moments were forever closed to him. He vaulted those hours in which he had already appeared. Time was able to prevent paradoxes; a moment once visited could never be seen again. He sensed the arrival of 1972 and felt it flowing gently past. He had stopped here once, a hot summer's day in Germany. Then 1971, 1970—years he also knew well. And 1969. These first Years of Madness—when the insanity that was to bring down the human race was only beginning the inexorable spiral which would end in sudden war and utter destruction—were his favorites; there was a sense of life in these times. What came afterward was unbearable.

And now it was 1968.

June 4, 1968.

Alfred opened his eyes. The ballroom swirled around him, filled with people. A young girl, pretty with auburn hair, dressed in a brief red-and-white garment, touched his arm.

"Where did you come from? I—"

"I'm fine," Alfred said. He hurried into the crowd, then stopped, raising a hand, and pretended to wave. *Click.* "Thank you," he called.

As midnight approached, Alfred found himself deliberately seeking the man with the scar. In the minutes he had already spent in the crowded ballroom—bright television lights turning the air as hot as midday—he had seen nothing, but soon he would leave, passing into a kitchen adjoining the ballroom —the actual site of the assassination—and he was certain he would find the scarred man there. His feet moved slowly as he walked through the crowd. Occasionally, he paused, snapping pictures, attempting to provide the professor with what he demanded: snapshots of the living, not the dead.

There was more room in the kitchen. Alfred breathed easily. Carefully, he turned and surveyed the people around him. The scarred man was not here. He recognized the assassin standing casually alone and snapped his picture. What would happen, he wondered, if he took action now, if he raised an alarm? But he didn't dare. No. Above all else, his father had drilled this into him: he was never to interfere with the inexorable progress of past events.

Someone beside him passed a cigarette. Alfred accepted gladly. The smoke tickled his throat. His mouth was dry from nervousness. From the ballroom, he heard a burst of excited cheering.

Maybe he wouldn't be here—the scarred man. There were times when Alfred thought the whole thing must be a private delusion: the man did not exist. Instead, he had been created —invented—from the faces of many men, transformed unconsciously into a single Satanic archetype.

But then Alfred saw him and all doubt was erased.

The man stood directly across a narrow corridor, softly speaking to the small dark figure Alfred had recognized as the future assassin. Shivering, Alfred turned away. Involuntarily, he raised a hand. *Click.* Another photograph to keep hidden: additional evidence of a truth he preferred never to know. *Click.*

The man stood beside him.

"Alfred."

"No." Raising his eyes, Alfred met the man's gaze briefly, seeing the deathly pale face, the scar which flickered brightly in the harsh white light.

"Don't you know me?"

"No," Alfred lied.

"Of course you do."

"No," Alfred said. Then: "Who are you?"

"A friend."

"No, what are you?"

"A man. Like you."

"Don't lie to me!" Alfred's voice, rising high, attracted angry glares; he was desecrating a moment of joyous celebration. From the ballroom came an excited voice booming through a loud-speaker. "I know who you are," Alfred said.

"Then tell me."

"You're the devil."

"Oh, come now." The man rocked on his heels, enjoying himself. "Really, Alfred. You needn't listen to that idiot and his book."

"The professor? You know him?"

"I know everyone. Here." He grabbed Alfred by the hand, his grip tight and unyielding. "Look at me. Come on—look close. You want to know? Here—see."

Alfred looked at the man. Once lost within those dark, swirling, utterly familiar eyes, there seemed to be no escape. He thought he was falling.

Drawing back, he blinked, then stared at the man, seeing him safely from without. "Why?" he cried.

"I thought you wanted to know."

"But you. No, no, no!"

"Yes," the other said softly.

"I'll kill you!"

"You can't." The crowd moved around them, surging aimlessly. "You forget. I know the future. Not only the past. I know tomorrow as well."

"But why?" cried Alfred.

The crowd was tearing them apart. Alfred fought to stay with the man. Then there were noises like firecrackers exploding in a chain. Alfred lost his balance, stumbled, fell. His camera slid out of his fingers, skidding across the floor. He crawled in pursuit.

People were screaming everywhere.

"But why show this to me?" asked Father Gordon, a plump, red-faced man dressed in flowing black robes. He stared at the photographs upon the table, shaking his head as if unable to accept the testimony of his own eyes.

"Who else?" asked Alfred.

THE AMBIGUITIES OF YESTERDAY   69

"Well, not me." Father Gordon's hands had begun to tremble. He hid them beneath the table, then tried to smile. "The professor—why not him? I merely assist when asked."

"But you have to sanctify his work. And he told me you do not accept his theory. I want to stop that book. Well, here's proof that it's a lie. If I let him see, he'd only say it showed him right."

"Of course," Father Gordon said, his stare fixed upon the table.

Alfred grabbed the photographs and tucked them in a pocket.

Father Gordon relaxed visibly. He asked, "Then you say it's not the devil after all."

"Of course it isn't. Didn't you hear me? I know this man. He's as human as I am."

"Well, then, who is he?"

Alfred lowered his voice to a whisper. "My son," he said.

"Oh, your son," Father Gordon said. He acted more irritated than amazed. Standing, he paced the length of the room, shaking his head violently, then made a sudden dash for the door.

Alfred caught his arm and held him. "I'm telling the truth. You have to help me. I should have known. Who else could travel freely through the past? It had to be him. But I want to know why."

"Ask him."

"I can't do that. He won't know—not until he does it. Then it'll be too late. How can I stop him?"

"You expect me to answer that?"

"You're one of God's representatives on Earth, aren't you?"

"I'm supposed to be." The priest dropped his eyes sadly. "So they say."

"Then tell me," Alfred said, no longer listening. "Help me." He shook the priest evenly. "You must."

"But I can't," said Father Gordon, jerking away. "My opinion is that you're overtaxed. You've been working too hard."

"Didn't you see the pictures?" Alfred asked softly.

"Yes."

"And wasn't it that same man?"

"Well, yes, I suppose it did look that way."

"Then who is he? What's your explanation?"

"Coincidence, perhaps," Father Gordon said.

Before Alfred could express his rage, the door flew open, revealing a cluster of figures. Alfred stepped back. They were children, barely in their teens, naked, filthy, shaggy: a gang.

"Father Gordon, run!" he cried.

But the priest did not move. He stood with his hands clasped, head lowered. In a gentle singsong voice, he murmured at the heavens.

Alfred stared at Father Gordon. "You—you brought them here."

"A mutant," the gang leader said, grinning. He was armed, clutching a knife carved from white bone in one fist. He crept into the room, the others following.

The priest continued to pray.

Lowering his head, Alfred dived forward. Grabbing the gang leader by the wrist, he twisted the knife from the boy's grasp. It struck the bare floor. Alfred fell on it.

Then the gang fell on him. He could feel their fingernails clawing at his clothes, tearing at his flesh like tiny knives. Over their harsh angry wails, the priest prayed louder and louder.

Alfred tucked the bone knife under his chest, clasping the handle, then shut his eyes. He searched the past calmly, seeking a convenient nook—some peaceful and pleasant time. Above him, the gang was screaming. He had heard enough.

He jumped.

Alfred watched the last photograph as the white edges curled inward, the brilliant center charred, and then the whole burst into flame.

Turning away from the fire, he walked easily across the room. The study was quite bare. It was night. He peered through the soiled window. Across the street in the empty house, a fire was burning. But he heard nothing, smelled nothing. He was alone.

In one hand, he held the bone knife. The tip was as sharp as a pin. He held it up, stroking the edge with his thumb, cutting his own flesh but feeling nothing.

Cautiously, he tiptoed down the hall, hearing the rising notes of his son's gentle breathing. He stepped slowly into the bedroom. A gas lantern, hanging behind, swept softly into the room, illuminating the pale face which lay upon the white pillow.

Alfred raised the knife and hurried ahead. Swiftly, he brought down the blade. He thought he could hear the sound of flesh tearing.

He stepped back.

Thomas sat up instantly, eyes open wide. For a moment, there was a clean wound—a white streak—then blood began to trickle down his face, soaking his bedclothes, dripping to the sheets and blankets.

The boy howled in pain.

Sickened, Alfred turned away. He should have known it

was not possible. The past was rigid, unchanging; there was nothing he could do but wait and wonder. He dropped the knife.

"Help me!" Thomas cried, holding his face. "It hurts! Oh, it hurts!"

"Yes," Alfred said. He hurried away, stumbling. "I'll help you," he called from the doorway. "It will be all right."

But he knew that was a lie. There would be a scar.

MINNA IN THE NIGHT SKY
Gail Kimberly

Minna Mantress hurried up the steps of Maple Heights private school, weaving her way through the milling crowds of teen-agers, and arrived at her second-floor classroom slightly out of breath and three minutes late. About half the class was there before her . . . fifteen pairs of eyes staring accusingly at her as she dropped her purse into her desk drawer and opened the lesson guide in front of her. She shouldn't be late, she knew that, but it was becoming increasingly harder for her to force herself to get here at all. She didn't look forward to her work these days. After twelve years of teaching, she had begun to believe she'd chosen the wrong profession. Oh, well . . . today just might be a good day after all, especially if Roger Pringle wasn't in class. She looked over the room, filling up now as more students straggled in the door, and saw that his seat was still empty. Not that it was only Pringle who caused her trouble, but he was one of the worst this semester.

"Yesterday we were discussing the Stamp Act," she began, "which was repealed in 1776 . . ."

"Hi, teacher!" The loud greeting was accompanied by the clunking of Roger Pringle's boots as he sauntered to his seat. Minna felt a tightening in her stomach. He was going to be awful again today. She could tell by his attitude.

"You're late, Roger," she said firmly. "Five minutes late."

"So were you," Roger said. "I saw you running up the stairs right after the bell went."

"Very well," Minna said. "If you're trying to imitate me, pick up some of my good qualities. Try learning history." A few of the students chuckled politely, but there was a current of tension in the class now and all of them could sense it.

Roger Pringle wasn't going to be outdone. "What for?" he said. "I don't care what happened before I was around. I want to know where the world is *going,* not where it's *been.* "

"Right on!" somebody called from the back of the class, and that started everybody talking at once.

Minna didn't even try to quiet them this time. She waited apprehensively, hoping she looked composed, remembering other days that had gone like this lately . . . too many of them. No use trying to tell herself that they were sixteen-year-old kids and she was twice their age. They didn't care about her age or her position as their teacher. Maybe that was her fault, or maybe it was the way kids today felt. Some of the other teachers in Maple Heights had confessed to feeling the same helplessness with their classes.

"Just what good is history, anyway?" Someone was shouting above the noise. Minna saw Jim Stickler, the one who was high on drugs most of the time, waving his hand. She started to answer him, but others were taking up the question, weaving it into a rhythmic chant, and she couldn't make herself heard. She listened to the shouts and the laughter, and saw the hostility in their faces, and in spite of herself she began to shake. She was close to tears, and she didn't want them to see that. She jumped up from her seat and held up her hands. "Quiet! Stop this noise!" But they were enjoying themselves too much to stop. Roger and some other boys were marching at the back of the room, and the rest of the class, with only one or two timid exceptions, was egging them on.

And then a man's voice boomed from the doorway. "What's going on here!"

Minna turned to see Mr. Justinian, the principal, standing there in red-faced outrage. The class suddenly quieted. Roger and his cohorts slipped quickly back into their seats. Mr. Justinian surveyed them coldly for a long moment before he turned to Minna. "Your class is disturbing the others." His voice was tight and cool. "We'd appreciate your keeping them quiet."

"I'm sorry," Minna said breathlessly.

Mr. Justinian came up to her desk and turned his back to the students so they wouldn't hear. "I want to see you in my office in your free period," he said, and then he left, but of course the whole class knew that Miss Mantress was in trouble now, and Minna knew she had lost what little hold she might ever have had on them. She tried to keep her voice from quivering. "We were discussing the Stamp Act," she said.

When she went to his office later, Mr. Justinian came right to the point. "Apparently teaching eleventh-graders is too hard a task for you, Miss Mantress. I'm sure you'll be able to find another teaching position, perhaps with younger children."

Minna felt suddenly ill. He was firing her! But she'd worked so hard! She'd tried to be a good teacher . . . never wanted to be anything else, not even a wife or a mother . . . and now, suddenly, he was telling her she *wasn't* a good teacher. Even the daily struggle with the students was preferable to this. She glared at his placid face. "I've taught here for twelve years! You can't just fire me like this! It's just that the kids nowadays don't want to learn . . . all of us have the same trouble with them!"

"By 'all of us' do you imply that all the teachers have the

same disciplinary problems you do?" He shook his head. "That isn't true. Most of the teachers run efficient classes of contented students. I'm sorry you're not one of them." He gave her a pitying smile. "There's more to teaching students than trying to cram knowledge into their heads, Miss Mantress. They're not machines."

Minna couldn't remember later just what else they said to each other, or how she got out of the school and into her car. The next thing she knew, she was racing down the freeway, clenching the steering wheel, her foot heavy on the accelerator. This wasn't the way home, but she didn't want to go home . . . to the apartment where nobody waited to ask how her day had been. It would be different if her mother were still alive, still living with her, and she could put this terrible, aching anger into words for someone who cared about her. No, she felt too alone now . . . too suddenly worthless and unneeded to face an empty apartment. She wanted to be with people. But there were no friends she could turn to. She'd never had time to make any close friends, and she'd never really needed any before.

After a while she found herself driving beside the beach, deserted on this April afternoon except for the sea gulls that circled above the waves and gathered on the rocks. She parked the car and walked on the sand, letting the cold breeze blow away some of her burning resentment, but it was lonely and she began to think how peaceful it could be to walk into those gently heaving waves and let them wash her, unresisting, out to sea. Good Lord, that was no answer to anything! One had to struggle on. Right now she knew she'd feel much better in a crowd. She hurried back to her car and drove on, and in a little while she saw the huge white skeleton that was the giant roller coaster and the dancing colored lights that decorated the

Tilt-A-Whirl and she could hear the music that sent the horses of the merry-go-round on their jogging race to nowhere. As she got out of the car, she could smell the hot dogs and the popcorn and she went, smiling, into the stream of people going onto the amusement pier.

She had always loved carnivals. The festival mood of the crowd was contagious, and she could never be unhappy there. The penny arcade blinked out excitement in flashing lights; the rides screamed thrills over the waters; the hall of mirrors echoed laughter. She hurried down a neon lane and bought a pink mountain of cotton candy and got it all over the end of her nose as she ate. She wasn't an adult any more, she was a child, and Mr. Justinian had never existed, and there was no Roger Pringle. A giant plaster man held his rocking belly and laughed outside the Fun House. She scurried over the whirling floors inside, and dodged the air jets that blew up her skirt, and even went down the slide at the exit, laughing. Goodness, it had been years since she'd done anything like this! She bought a hot dog and ate it on the merry-go-round, and the sea winds blew all the curl out of her hair.

Then it grew late, the crowd thinned, the winds turned cruel, and her feet were tired. Minna leaned against a wall by the deserted rifle gallery. It was all coming back . . . the anger and the frustration and the realization that she had lost too much . . . more starkly real now that it had simmered in her subconscious for hours. That Justinian was a bastard! The word gave her satisfaction and she said it out loud as she took off a shoe and rubbed the aching toes of her left foot. "Bastard!"

There was a face in the darkness near her, and a voice that said: "I beg your pardon?" Minna, startled, jammed her foot back into her shoe and started to walk away, but the man put his hand on her arm. "Were you talking to me?"

"No," Minna said. "I wasn't talking to anybody." She could see him now, in the lights of the rifle gallery, a tall, bearded man wearing a red sweater over a white shirt and pants. He looked familiar, but she didn't know why. Perhaps she'd seen him before somewhere. He spoke gently, and his eyes and his hand on her arm were gentle, too. "I thought you might be a customer," he said. "I haven't had any tonight."

Minna looked behind him and saw, for the first time, a small door in the wall she had leaned against. Lettered across it were the glowing white words: KNOW THE PAST AND THE FUTURE.

"Do you tell fortunes?"

"Of course not," he said. "It's a ride, like the roller coaster or the merry-go-round."

"That little door?"

"Well, you have to go through it. The ride's behind the door." He pushed it open, and Minna hesitated only a moment before her curiosity made her go through, and then they were in a vast sky of midnight blue where stars shimmered around them. Minna wondered for a moment what they were standing on, but it felt solid enough under her feet. "Is this it?" she asked, feeling a bit dizzy.

"Oh, no. This is just for atmosphere. Twinkle lights over dark blue cloth on the walls and ceiling."

"Then where's the ride?"

He must have turned on a switch then, because a light came on in the center of the sky, and in the light was a big glass globe with a chair and a small table inside. The table looked like a control panel, all knobs and dials. "For time travel," he said.

"Of course," Minna said uneasily. "For time travel. Well, it doesn't look like much fun, and I was just on my way home . . ." She wondered what had ever made her come in here in the first place.

"You don't believe me," the man said sadly. "They never do." He walked over to the globe and stood in the light. "It's quite real, you know. I invented it myself a few years ago. Very safe and entirely foolproof. Would you like to go to the future? See what life will be like, say, five hundred years from now?"

"You're right," Minna said firmly. "I don't believe you."

"Would you, if you saw my certificates, diplomas, degrees? I've got a B.S. and a Ph.D. and all sorts of impressive credentials in physics and engineering."

"You carry them around with you?" Minna said.

"No, they're in my office back there." He waved past the globe toward the twinkling stars. "I'll bring them out and show you."

"That's all right," Minna said. "I don't need to see them."

"But you're still not ready for the ride?"

"If you really have a time machine, or whatever you call it, why is it hidden away here in an amusement park? Why hasn't anyone ever heard of it? Why hasn't such a great scientific discovery been used for important purposes?" She wasn't going to stand here much longer. Her feet still hurt, and this was obviously a ridiculous situation. The man was harmless, but she should never have come in here.

"The usual good questions." He walked back to stand beside her. "The answer is greed. My own greed. This is my invention and I want to make money from it. And I do. But I won't sell it and I certainly won't donate it to science. They'd all love to get their hands on it if they knew, but first thing you know it would belong to the government and they'd use it for their own purposes. I wouldn't be able to use it myself any more. And besides being greedy, I'm an altruist in my own way.

I feel the purpose of this time traveler is to help people who need help. They come to me by the dozens, you know . . . some recommended by psychiatrists of my acquaintance . . . some hear about it through the grapevine . . . some come in accidentally, as you did." His voice was soothing and almost hypnotic. "I think you need help, Mrs. . . . uh . . ."

"Miss Mantress. Minna Mantress. I get the feeling I've seen you somewhere before."

"I'm Grant Roan." He studied her face in the dimness. "I don't think we've ever met, but I know you're unhappy, aren't you? I could tell that the minute I saw you. Life isn't being kind to you, is it, Miss Mantress?"

"No." Minna heard her voice crack. "It certainly isn't." It was his sympathy, his interest, that made her say it.

"But the future, where life is different and people are different . . ."

"The past," Minna said.

"But the excitement of the future . . ."

"I teach history," Minna said.

"The past, then. What time will you have? 1776? 1890? 1900? I don't like to send anyone back more than two hundred years unless they really insist. The change is entirely too drastic for most people."

Minna pictured herself in front of a class of prim children, the girls in gingham skirts, hair tied back with precise bows; the boys in knickers and stiff-collared shirts, their eager minds untainted by TV or movies or drugs, waiting to hear the history of their country and the world. She looked suddenly at Grant Roan and saw his gaze on her, as though he knew her thoughts. "It's not real, is it?" she said.

"It's very real indeed, and it's yours for the asking, and, say, a thousand-dollar fee."

"A thousand dollars!"

His smile was charming. "I told you I was greedy. But to go back to the past . . . isn't that worth a thousand or more?"

Minna went over to the glass globe and put her hands on its cold, smooth curve. The chair inside was thickly padded in white plastic and there were slightly worn spots on it, as though it had been used many times. The globe shimmered like a bubble against the background of blackness, and Roan's soft voice behind her said: "The past is your home, Miss Mantress. Think of it. Peaceful and safe. What are you afraid of in a time you know so well?"

"I'm not afraid." She stepped suddenly through the opening in the globe and sat down in the chair.

"Well?" He smiled in at her. "What year would you like?"

Minna lay back against the padding and closed her eyes. "1886," she said. "That was a good time."

"I'll take a check for the thousand," Roan said, "and you can leave right now."

Minna's eyes popped open and she stood up. "I wish it were real," she said, brushing past him, stepping out into the starry night sky. "I wish it were true," she said wistfully. "How do I get out of here?"

He led her back to the door. "What are you going home to?" he asked her.

Minna thought of Mr. Justinian and Roger Pringle and the empty apartment. She was afraid of them, not of the past. She was afraid to start all over again with a new school and a new principal and a new set of students, that is, if she could get another teaching job. That might take months, and she was afraid of that, too . . . the waiting, the hoping, and the agonizing loneliness. She looked back to the bubble, shimmering in the light, and then she was walking back toward it, and seating herself in the white chair, and writing out a check, and Roan was leaning over the control panel, setting the dials.

"Can I get back if I want to?" Minna asked him. "Don't you have to prepare me somehow before I go? Will I be the same when I get to 1886 as I am now, or will I change?"

He turned away from the control board and stepped out of the glass globe. "Remember, I'll be here," he said.

"What?" Minna said, but the globe was whirling like a tumbleweed, and she seemed to be whirling, too, although she had no sense of falling. This lasted only a minute or so and then the globe was still, but Grant Roan was gone, and the night sky was the real night sky that hung over an empty beach. She stood up and went out onto the cold sand. A line of gold along the horizon showed that the sun would soon be rising, and in the half-light she could see gulls perched on a rock formation nearby. But nothing seemed any different. Had the machine only whirled her out onto the beach? She turned around and saw that it had disappeared.

She walked across the sand, her heart beating hard, up a little rise to where the highway should be, but there was no highway, and there were no stores or hamburger stands or gas stations or cars or oil derricks, only stretches of open fields just visible in the faint light. And there was a house, isolated on a rise a short distance away.

She headed for it, seeing a light shining through one of the windows, thinking of what she would say if there was no trickery and this really was 1886. She would tell them she was lost and wanted a ride to the nearest town, and then she would go to a hotel and after a while she'd find a school where she could teach, or maybe even start a school if the town didn't already have one. The thought excited her so that she almost ran up the rutted lane that led to the front yard, and then up the front steps. A scent of baking bread came through the open window. She knocked on the door. For some reason the sound was very faint, so she knocked harder, paining her knuckles against the wood. They still made only a faint sound. There must be something wrong with the door.

She shouted "Hello!" through the open window. She could hear someone moving around inside, but her call got no response so she called again, and after a few minutes she decided they couldn't hear her. There must be a back door. She walked around the side of the house, seeing a clothesline stretched between two trees and a swing hanging from a tree branch and an old-fashioned doll with a wooden head lying in the weeds.

Just as she saw the back door, it opened and a little girl came out. She was about seven, wearing a long white nightgown, with her long brown hair in tangles down her back.

"Hello there!" Minna said, but the child didn't seem to see her or hear her. She left the door ajar as she ran barefoot into the yard and picked up the doll. Minna went up to the door and looked inside, into a big kitchen where a woman was standing by a wood stove, cooking. The wooden floor of the room was bare, and a crudely made wooden table and four chairs stood to one side.

"Hello!" Minna called to the woman, who didn't even glance at her, so Minna went inside, repeating her greeting. At that moment the child came running back inside, slamming the door behind her, and Minna had to move quickly to avoid being run into as the girl ran to the table, sat down, and began straightening the doll's clothes. The woman turned then and spoke to the child, and Minna felt fear cold in her stomach. The woman had looked right through her. Neither she nor the child could see her standing there. Minna went right up to her and shouted at her, and waved a hand in front of her face, but the woman didn't even blink. Frightened, Minna tried the same thing with the little girl, and when there was no reaction, she tried to knock over an empty chair, but she was unable even to move it, no matter how she tried. It was the same when she pulled at one of the window curtains. It didn't even wrinkle in her clenching hand. After a while, a man and another little girl came into the room, but Minna found it was the same thing with them. Then she tried opening the door to leave, but her fingers couldn't budge it. Frantic, she ran through the little house, pushing things and pulling them, shouting and screaming and even crying, but at last she knew that she did not exist in this time and there was only one thing for her to do. Go back.

But how? What had that man said to her? "I'll be here." Where? He must have known what would happen and that she'd be looking for a way to get back. But where was "here?" It must be the beach . . . the place the globe had taken her. In the future that spot would be Roan's place on the amusement pier.

She had to wait until the man opened the door and then she slipped outside and walked back to the beach. On the way she saw a lone man driving a horse and buggy, and she stood right in his path and waved to him, but when he almost ran her down, looking through her with unseeing eyes, she knew it was completely useless.

It took her quite a while to find the strange rock formation. There was no sign of the globe or of Roan, and so she curled up on the damp sand, exhausted, and slept.

Roan's voice woke her. She opened her eyes and he was standing over her, smiling.

"You!" She wanted to jump up and slap his face, but she was too stiff to move quickly, and when she tried to get up, she discovered her legs hurt, so she sat on the sand and hated him.

He kept on smiling. "It wasn't much fun, was it? You've had a bad time. Still, if I'd told you before you came to the past, you wouldn't have believed me, would you?" He reached out his hand to help her get up. "And I didn't leave you stranded."

"But I don't understand. This *is* 1886, isn't it? I'm here, in this time, but nobody sees me."

"Come on," he said, leading her into the glass globe. "I'll explain it all when we get back and you get something to eat."

It was a short trip back to the starry night sky room, and Minna realized that she was just as hungry as she was angry and disappointed, but she let Grant Roan take her to a restaurant on the pier and order bacon, eggs, and coffee for her.

"The future is frightening to most people," he told her as she ate, "but the past seems safe. That's why I didn't try to tell you what would happen once you were there. I let you find out for yourself, and now you know the time traveler works, and you know I keep my word, so you'll want to try the future, and you'll be willing to pay me five thousand dollars to send you there." He grinned at her over his coffee cup. "Remember my greed."

Minna nearly choked on her food. "Five thousand dollars! What makes you think I'd pay that?"

"Because the present is still the wrong time for you, and now you know you can't live in the past. The future . . . that's where you belong."

"But why was it that nobody could see or hear me?"

"The past has already happened," Roan said, "and you didn't exist then. You were seeing 1886, but you weren't there and you couldn't influence it in any way."

"But I *was* there!"

"Not when it was happening, you weren't. It's over and

done with now, like a picture that's already been painted. None of us have any place there. Observe . . . yes. Influence it . . . no."

"It was a frustrating feeling."

"Then try the future."

"No."

"Look, you don't even have to pay me unless you're completely satisfied."

"What do you mean?"

"I'll meet you in whatever future year you choose, a little while after you get there. If you're not completely satisfied to be there, I'll bring you back to the present. If you are, I get my five thousand."

Minna looked at his sympathetic, honest eyes and his charming smile. "A salesman," she said, shaking her head. "That's what you are. A real salesman. You'd think you were selling me a used car."

He shrugged. "I'm selling you a new life. Think of me more as a psychiatrist. . . ."

"And will I exist in the future?"

"Of course. It hasn't yet happened, so you can be quite important in it."

"I don't think I understand all this," Minna said, shaking her head, but in the end she agreed to go five hundred years into the future.

The time traveler stopped its whirling on the beach and Minna got out, only this time there were no gulls, but people playing in the surf and sitting on the rock formation. They crowded around her and spoke to her. "How great you could come," one of them said into her ear. "You're needed here," another said to her.

Then they led her away to a vehicle that looked like a giant dragonfly, with a shimmering body and four gauzy wings. Three of them accompanied her while they soared over the sea and landed on a mountainside, and there she was coaxed out and escorted through flowered gardens and into a building that seemed to be part of the mountain. They showed her rooms that looked out over the sea, richly furnished and stocked with books, music tapes, closets of clothing . . . and told her this was where she would live.

"You won't be lonely," one of the women told her. "There are some others here like you."

Minna didn't understand until the next day.

Grant Roan came several days later, and found her in one of the shady courtyards near a fountain. She was just sitting there, looking contented, and when she saw him, she only smiled.

"You *are* happy here, then?" he asked her.

"And if I wasn't? Would you really take me back in your time traveler?"

"No," he said. "I couldn't do that. We need you here, but we wanted to make sure you'd come of your own accord and that when you got here, you'd want to stay."

"You knew about me before I went to the amusement pier, didn't you? It must be your job, to recruit teachers. I finally figured that out."

"Yes, I learned all about you and even followed you around for several weeks. We wanted you very much. Your kind of dedication to teaching isn't common."

"But how did you know I'd go to the amusement pier?"

"I would have arranged to be wherever you were at the right time," he said. "And my job isn't such a bad one. You look happy enough."

"I've met the other three teachers here, of course." She twirled a crimson blossom in her fingers. "Art. Literature. Biology. And now me, for history. Will you bring any more?"

"Oh, yes, and there are other human teachers here now, in other places. We have to learn as much as you can teach us. When humans invented us, they didn't think we'd need to know about such things as fine arts. They programmed us to perform our tasks, and that was all, not knowing we'd survive after they were gone. Now we want to rebuild their civilization."

"I can hardly believe you're *not* human," Minna said.

"Externally, we're good copies. Humans all died out more than three hundred years ago. Pollution killed off all the life forms eventually, until only we were left. Androids don't need clean air or clean water."

"You're all such good students." Minna suddenly laughed.

"What's so funny?" Grant Roan asked her.

"Machines!" she said, but she wouldn't explain to him any further.

WAIF
Fritz Leiber

I was sitting at my typewriter at Venice, California, in my tiny, bedraggled house at eight o'clock in the morning. Through the window, which was finely filmed by smoke, dust, and grease and imprinted by our cat Selim's nose, I saw a medium heavy fog that made nearby buildings dim low rectangles, the street a wide, cottony path; I knew there was a white line down the middle, but I couldn't see it.

Everything was still as death.

Which was good and proper for my wife in the other room. Estelle gets her deep sleep in the mornings, after restless or wakeful nights. She has terrors in darkness and then grows calm with the dawn.

Even the ocean, two blocks away, couldn't be heard. Though its surf, light or loud, is never anything but a lovely embroidery on what silence there may be.

Beside me, a wisp of steam still rose from a half cup of black coffee and there smoldered a half cigarette, and from it rose a lazier curve of smoke.

The silence continued, unusual even for Venice and almost beginning that sort of tension where the ticking of a distant clock becomes artillery and one begins to listen for one's heart.

Most outsiders, even the rest of those in Los Angeles, think of Venice as a wild and dangerous place, noisy with blacks and chicanos and their protestings, rackety with beatniks and hippies and their street music and riots and arrests, wailing with winos, screaming bloody murder with street fights and rapes, screeching with the punished tires of lawless, chain-draped motorcycle gangs or those of dope pushers' cars fleeing pursuing police. Could be, but the sounds I've chiefly heard in my many years here have been soft conversation, the distant strumming of a guitar, the occasional screech of a sea gull, the faint thud of oil wells in back yards and on the beach, and the almost unhearable thrum of the tires of squad cars softly cruising along wide Ocean Front Walk, forbidden even to bicycles, between the low buildings and the sand.

Maybe the socially nasty sounds are kept away from me, by chance or my unconscious, but my notion is that Venice is dying and its silence that of the deathbed—or that of the death cell, an area of Los Angeles doomed by the forces that want to mash it flat and replace it with towering high-rise apartments and vast areas of asphalted parking space, the entire link between past and future gone, the present somehow completely vanished, and forgotten forever the fairy city of canals built in 1905 by Abbott Kinney, who hasn't now even a gravestone of his own, but only one empty street a half block long bearing his last name.

These were death thoughts, I realized, or fog thoughts, as I sat with motionless hands before my typewriter.

Yet sea fog was the reason the forces wanted Venice. It meant that nine times out of ten the west wind was blowing back the smog of Los Angeles and replacing it with relatively pure marine air. Which made the land here potentially more profitable than that, say, of the San Fernando Valley, darling of suburbs in the 1930's but now a soup plate of smog.

I drained half the coffee remaining in my cup, took the last drag of my cigarette, stubbed it out, and looked once more at the fog. It was thicker, if anything, completely shrouding the higher outlines of the Home for the Wanted, a progressive orphanage founded anonymously by Abbott Kinney and still continued by Los Angeles, largely on the basis of private contributions.

The silence continued intense. I listened for my wife's breathing in the other room and didn't hear a thing. It was strange that a car hadn't come by in the last few minutes—or was it only seconds? Anyhow, I began to get that feeling of being the last man in the world, which isn't at all bad when you know your wife is sleeping peacefully nearby. But what if she should be dead?

I shook my head to clear it and my fingers to supple them. I lit another cigarette. I lifted my hands.

And now I was—perhaps—going to shatter the continuing intense silence with the staccato blat of my typewriter. But that was the one sound which wouldn't waken my wife. She would know it meant I was happy and working, and that would only make her sleep deeper.

I hesitated. It was hard to decide what to start on. In my mind were thunderings and explosions, about an article on the generation gap and one on pollution, and several short stories, and this and that and everything, in fact, the entire universe or universes. But all this cannonade stirred not a grain of dust nor a delicate curl of cigarette smoke. As they say, "Silent as thought."

But then my mind grew deathly silent, too. Something— Estelle close beyond the flimsy wall, old guilts, the fog silent and beautiful as the stars—made me think of our daughter Lynn, dead at the age of twelve—eleven years ago—of an obscure heart ailment. For the thousandth time I told myself that if

Lynn had lived, Estelle would still have an occupation, or at least a concern, or perhaps gone naturally on to another occupation, instead of feeding on me alone, which made me feed on her, and she giving way to grief, then boredom, and finally terror, so that she never felt safe except with two bolts, a chain, and the lock on the front and only door. Perhaps I should have taken her away from Venice, but I'm a slow mover.

These thoughts, too, made me start to remember an old guilt I tried to fight down, not even to know about.

At my ear, at last breaking the silence, a soft girlish voice said, "Hey, mister, I've found your cat."

I jerked around, spilling the dregs of my coffee on the floor and losing my cigarette. After fumble-finding the latter, I slowly looked up.

She wasn't at my ear, but halfway to the front doorway. She was a slim girl about eleven or twelve years old. She had low black shoes, black stockings or pantyhose, a pale gray mini dress. Gently clutched to her tummy was our cat Selim, who managed to remain dignified even in this situation—a grave, thoughtful-eyed male who looked both sleek and battle-scarred.

My first reaction was that the girl was my dead daughter Lynn come back. But then I saw that her hair was black, not brown, her face thinner and more tapering, her eyes violet and larger and coolly inspecting, not green and shyly peering, her mouth wider than Lynn's.

She smiled and said, "He was 'way down the street."

My second reaction was sexual attraction. Her smile made her seem years older. Her figure and dress fitted that, too, especially her long, black-sleeved legs. The twin swellings at her bosom might be small, developing breasts—or else a foam-rubber-padded brassiere perhaps provided by a mother who thought her daughter couldn't become erotically attractive early enough.

What was I doing with a desire like this when my wife was sleeping on the other side of the wall?

For that matter, considering the laws of the land, what legal thing could I do with some girl at most a year or so over twelve?

And what was I thinking of having any aggressive intentions at all toward a girl who returned me my cat?

But how could I have such intentions in any case?—for now she seemed to me simply a creature of the fog, despite her smile. A waif in shades of gray, something from another realm, despite her human speech and appearance? Something impalpable, untouchable. But with what a sweet visage.

And then I got the fourth of my reactions, but stronger—that this girl was not dead Lynn or some strayed nymphet, but someone I had known and known and known—to an unendurable degree. But that was only a shadow memory. Yet somehow the girl halfway between me and the door now seemed dangerous—a sinister figure from another planet.

She let down Selim onto the floor. He strode dignifiedly toward the farther end of the room, where his eating, drinking, and toilet facilities were.

My fears vanished. Now that Selim was gone, I saw that my little girl was wearing around her slim middle a black plastic belt carrying a black plastic toy pistol in a black plastic holster.

She was a Girl Adventurer, out on mornings as well as evenings. Probably going to school right now.

Taking an easy step toward me, she said, "Selim was more than two blocks away when I found him, Mr. Andre."

Her voice was not reproachful, only factual.

I did not tell her Selim was a free cat and could rove as many blocks as he pleased. "Thanks for finding him," I said.

"How did you know my name is Andre—and his Selim, for that matter?"

She said, "I've heard you calling him Selim. And your wife calling you. I live with the Fosters, three houses up. They're not my real Poppa and Momma. My Momma died when I was born and my Poppa went away. I was brought up in the Home for the Wanted. Then they put me with the Fosters two months ago."

"Did the Fosters give you that charming dress?"

She smiled. "I made it. They taught me a little sewing at the Home and I went on from there."

I was suddenly struck with mild guilt or uneasiness at passing even mild compliments to a sub-adolescent girl child alone with me. Estelle is forever warning me against such situations. Mostly I think she's silly, but sometimes I think she's half right, considering the society in which we spend our days, with its queer mixture of freedom and puritanism, its tendency to translate all body contacts and privacies into sexual ones.

"You'd better get on to school, hadn't you?" I said lamely, "or you'll be late."

Her eyes twinkled and she laughed softly. "It doesn't matter. They still haven't decided whether to put me into fourth grade or jump me to seventh. I read in the little library."

"Uh, kiddo—" I started. It didn't sound right. "What's your name, if I may ask?" Which sounded much too grown-up, I told myself. Or did it?

"They call me Sophy."

"Well, Sophy, what did they teach you at the Home besides sewing?"

"I helped look after the littler kids. When I got a chance, I'd sneak away to the beach and look at the ocean and make up things. On clear nights I'd go up on the roof and look at the stars and imagine what sort of worlds are up there. Worlds of cats with no people, worlds where spaceships are buses you take every hour to some other planet, worlds ruled by children who never grow up, worlds of flowers, water worlds with wise porpoises, worlds where wishes always work, worlds—"

I might have listened to her all morning, except I heard Estelle move in the bedroom and cringed at the row she might make.

So I interrupted softly, "That's nice, Sophy, but now I've got to get to work and you've got to get to school." I turned to my typewriter and made a big thing of poising my hands over the keys.

"Can I come again?" Her low voice was receding.

I nodded briefly and clattered out, "Now is the time for all good men to come to the aid of the party" and "The quick brown fox jumped over the lazy dog."

When I looked up, the girl was gone and Selim had come from his end of the room and was peering around.

I opened the bedroom door in slow motion, artful to avoid its two creaks. Estelle was still sleeping. She had just changed position. I closed the door the same way.

Then I moved to the front door and felt a little shiver as I saw that all the bolts and chains were locked.

The shiver didn't last long. Beside the door the tall, narrow window was open, with only an easy three-foot drop to the lawn, which wouldn't show footprints in any case. An unconventional entry, but then, an unconventional girl.

So I stopped thinking of Sophy whisking off through the roof to the stars, but skipping to school instead through the thinning fog.

As if to emphasize the point, Selim gave me a look I judged to be contemptuous and sprang out the window without even touching its sill.

Still, Sophy stayed on my mind all day, or more precisely on the top of my subconscious. I was concerned at the depth of my first reactions to her, especially in the sexual area.

That afternoon I spent some time at the Santa Monica Library, boning up on the Roman Republic for a novel I might set there. When I got home, Estelle and Sophy were having tea and thin sandwiches together. Estelle is English.

I wasn't really surprised at Sophy coming back so soon, but I was at how well she and Estelle seemed to be getting along. Veddy ladylike, both of them.

Sophy stood up, nodded slightly toward me, and gave me the ghost of a curtsy. Veddy British, indeed. From another century.

At that moment a hell peculiar to the owners of cats and dogs broke loose.

Black hair on end so he looked three times his size, Selim bounded in through the tall, open window, closely followed by a huge, tall, skinny brown dog, jaws agape, who looked a mix of hound, police dog, and Mexican hairless.

They circled the room twice like hairy comets, one of them mangy—Estelle clutching her tea service, me slow to react as usual—and shot into the bedroom.

Sophy, moving coolly, was at the bedroom door ahead of me. Through the yips and snarls I heard a sharp little click. Then all sounds ceased. I looked around quickly. Selim was standing on the tousled bed, still like a green-eyed porcupine in battle array. But the big brown dog was nowhere.

"He went out that way," Sophy told me, pointing at the bedroom window. "You should have seen him scramble."

The window was open less than a foot at the bottom. Still, he had been a very scrawny dog, despite his height.

"I bet people have shot at him before and he knows guns soon as he spots them," Sophy said. She presented her little black plastic pistol sidewise, close to my face. I saw it didn't even have a hole in the muzzle, which was flat, unbroken plastic like the rest. "I clicked it and he beat it." She returned the toy to its black holster. Then she advanced to pick up Selim.

"Don't," I said. "You can't handle him when he's like that. He once gave me a bite a half inch deep when I tried."

"Andre had to have tetanus shots," Estelle supplemented over my shoulder. "Don't try."

Sophy picked up the bristling Selim. There were no bites, scratches, growls, yowls, or squirmings. She sat down on the edge of a chair in the living room with Selim on her lap. In a couple of minutes his hair was down and he was purring. We mostly stared at her and didn't speak.

She put him down with a final caress and stood up.

She said, "Well, I must be going now or the Fosters will be wondering. Thanks so much for the tea, Mrs. de Leon."

And she went out the door to the street. No windows or mysterious vanishings.

About an hour later Estelle remarked, "You know, Andre, Sophy reminds me of how Lynn was when she died. Or how Lynn would have been."

I nodded after a bit. "About the same age."

"She's very interested in you," Estelle went on matter-of-factly. "She already knew you were a writer. She wanted to know if you turned out science fiction and fantasy. She was a little disappointed when I told her, no, historical novels and articles on social stuff and anthropology."

"You used a big word like that?"

"She took it in her stride." Estelle smiled a slightly crooked smile. "You know, she looks a little like you."

I suppressed a guffaw. Estelle becomes resentful when her slightest opinion is questioned or, still worse, ridiculed, even obliquely.

The smile grew crookeder. "What's more, she has a crush on you."

I smiled, but once more I did the suppression bit, this time of a groan. Estelle believes that every female from eighteen months to eighty years plus has a crush on me. Even if she makes friends with them all by herself, I steal them away from her as soon as I see them.

I never disagree unless I lose my temper. One doesn't question the absolutes or someone one loves, whatever shape the love or the absolutes may take.

After dinner Estelle resumed, but on a different tack.

"Sophy told me she hasn't been adopted by the Fosters. They just get a little money from the Home for taking care of her." She paused and looked sidewise at me without the crooked smile—indeed, she seemed wistful, tentative.

"Do you think, Andre, we could possibly adopt her? She'd be like Lynn, come again. Maybe she was even conceived the moment Lynn was dying. Oh, I know you would be the main attraction, even though she does like playing high tea. But I could sop up the overflow, and she would give me something to occupy myself."

The mixture of selfishness and tolerance in that almost cool little speech stopped me. Also, I felt a sudden mysterious twinge of guilt different from any of my other feelings about Sophy, even that disturbing sexual angle. Offhand, I guessed it referred to something I'd sunk so deep and heavy-weighted into my subconscious that even its shadow hadn't obtruded into my conscious mind. Though completely masked, it bothered me sharply.

To Estelle I temporized, "That'll take a lot of thinking about. After all, we're middle-aged, have been for a few years."

Estelle said, "Sophy told me the Fosters are each of them seventy or more. As for Sophy, I'd do the taking care of."

"Still, it would take a lot of thinking." That strange new pinpoint of unknown guilt was still thrusting into me.

"Think about something and you don't do it," Estelle said quickly, giving me a look of cynical contempt. "But think about it anyhow. Nice to have a slim, pre-nubile maiden around the house, eh?" she added with a slight smile as mirthless as a madam's.

"And nice for you to have a doll to dress up and play with," I was tempted to add, but of course didn't.

Later that evening I strolled down to the empty beach to look at the small white breakers coming in through the black like troops of children's ghosts. Overcast hid all the stars, Venice's old street lights were unobtrusive, there was no sound but the gentle yet always shiversome surf and the west wind cool and steady and humming faintly like a seashell held to my ear.

Trudging home, a shade tired from footing it through the loose sand, I noticed Norman Saylor sitting on his front steps a few doors from ours smoking a smelly pipe. At his lazy wave I joined him and half in self-protection lit a harsh cigarette myself.

Norman is in his sixties, a retired professor of sociology and anthropology. Very bright, almost a great mind in his day, but uncompetitive and lazy. I think he does a lecture now and then and even writes an occasional paper and still gets it reputably published, but mostly he just rails genially at the world he helped to create in his revolutionary, actively anti-establishment days and loafs around and wanders the beach and re-explores his books. His library is a bit bigger than his house, but somehow he keeps the volumes from coming out the windows or completely blocking the doors. Naturally he is a godsend to me when I get hung up on knotty points in my articles—or my novels, too, for that matter. And most fortunately he doesn't think being a godsend amounts to a hill of beans.

He fetched us a couple of tall, big, stiff highballs and pretty soon I was telling him the works about Sophy.

"That sex-attraction angle is interesting," he interrupted once. "From the silent way Sophy came and went, and from her air of cool command—something I guess at from the things you say and don't say—she might be your Anima."

"Anima?" I said. "That's some idea of Jung's, isn't it? One of the Archetypes. The female . . ." I trailed off, my own ideas and knowledge uncertain."

"Uh-huh," Norman responded. "Each man's female self, existing in the subconscious a level or so below what Jung calls the Shadow—another Archetype. She appears to a man in dreams and sometimes in fantasies and hallucinations and sometimes she merely makes her lovely and—yes—terrible presence felt to him. She is generally a beautiful woman, though she can appear as a hag. She's really more goddess than woman, inspiring a man's creativity and other urges: imperious, fierce, idealistic yet utterly realistic, sometimes whimsical, and merciless toward a man who fails her, meaning a man who is cowardly or flinches from producing the best that's in him.

"For of course, as you know very well, she's no real woman or goddess, but a man's concept of what such a goddess-woman would be. Someone to inspire him, someone to adore. An essence of femininity forever pulling him out and away, first from his mother, then from his wife—though both his wife and mother have entered greatly into her make-up. And she's always linked with the wild and the mysterious and the infinitely distant."

"That's odd," I said. "While I was alone with Sophy this morning, I distinctly got the notion that she hadn't come by door or window, but straight from the stars. By transporter maybe, like the *Enterprise*. Ridiculous, isn't it?"

At that moment Norman took a deep draw on his new-filled pipe, and by its glow I saw his usually sardonic lips curl upward in a brief, but genuine, grin.

"Another odd thing, to use your first adjective, not your second," he said. "It happens—maybe you know it—that Jung was very much interested in space flight and other worlds, something that made more conservative psychoanalysts consider him (privately, of course) an eminent crackpot, a somewhat flawed bigwig, high in their hierarchy—one of the big three with Freud and Adler—but not (in some areas) taken seriously. Jung even dug flying saucers, though he appears to have thought of them as significant mental projections rather than actual vehicles.

"He even read and valued science fiction. He thought— and stated in his books for his colleagues to read and maybe shake their heads at—that the best fictional representations of the Anima were She in H. Rider Haggard's book, L'Atlantide in the Frenchman's novel of that name, and Selene in William Sloane's *To Walk the Night*. You'll recall Selene came from the stars and had to kill her two Earth husbands against her will before she went back to the stars."

"Very interesting," I commented somewhat noncommittally. I'd heard most of that part of his talk before, but one doesn't voice such things if one hopes to keep friends.

At the same time I felt a little shiver. Venice does get dark once you're a little bit off the infrequent boulevards, and there weren't even the garish lights of a small liquor store in sight. Twice I felt impelled to look up for stars while fearing to see them, silly as that may sound, but the sky was still completely overcast. Good to be sitting by Norman with a little of my drink left.

He went on. "Jung says that a young man usually has a mature, or somewhat more than mature, woman for an Anima. For a middle-aged man she takes the form of a girl *Playboy* might feature or someone a little older—no bunny, though, but a young goddess. While an elderly man is apt to have a little girl for an Anima, perhaps accounting for child molestation by the proto-senile. I hardly think of you as middle-aged, Andre, so Sophy seems a little young for your Anima."

"I don't know," I said. "Sometimes I feel awfully old."

He chuckled. "Well, now you've got a nymphet Anima, halfway between child and young goddess. Just remember, young or old, she's equally powerful."

He fetched us another highball and we chatted of other things.

After a bit I said suddenly, "My God, it's late. Estelle will be frightened. Probably already is."

As I eased his little yard-gate shut, Norman called after me softly but with his customary raillery, "Hey, Andre, don't take seriously any of that guff I told you about the Anima. Jung was never much of anything but a prose poet, and a very ponderous one."

Late next afternoon Sophy paid us another visit. Estelle invited her to stay to dinner. Sophy said the Fosters wouldn't mind, and she was so certain and mature about it that we didn't check with the Fosters, something I'm sure we'd have done in the case of any other child.

It was a lovely meal. Estelle outdid herself—tender steak-

and-kidney pie with crispy crust that almost melted in your mouth, peas and tiny new potatoes, mixed salad, chocolate pudding with whipped cream. There were no apparent constraints among the three of us. We were like three congenial adults, yet Sophy remained a child—paradoxical, but true.

"I wish we could always do this," Estelle said at last, settling back with a cigarette and broaching the matter closest to her heart.

I nodded before I realized I'd done so. Dammit, I'd better watch out or I'd be committing myself to the adoption project.

Sophy said, "It *has* been nice. Like three cats having dinner."

"I don't know about that," I said, "I've known some cats were hellers. No table manners at all."

"I mean civilized cats," Sophy explained.

"The cats you told me lived up in the sky?" I asked.

"On a cat-size planet circling a sun," she corrected me with gentle pedantry.

Estelle said, her eyes dreamy with brandy and unfulfillment, "I'd like to live in the sky forever. Just lie on a cloud and float and dream."

"I don't think you're a sky person, Mrs. de Leon," Sophy observed, so obviously absorbed in thought no one could have taken offense. "You like a room better than room."

This child-epigram went unnoticed because both Estelle and I realized how true it was. At any rate Estelle's eyes flickered toward the other room, where she did spend much of her time in bed with a book and a bottle.

She rallied by asking Sophy, "Didn't you ever have a favorite room?"

"Oh, yes, the little one in the Home on the third floor near the ladder to the roof. It made it easy to go up and look at the stars."

That made it easy to talk about Sophy's early childhood. It turned out her mother hadn't died exactly when she was born, but when she was about three, though her father had been out of the picture from the start.

"I don't remember him myself at all, but I do remember a lot about my mother, though the psychologist from the Home told me I was just imagining, especially when I told him she taught me things about the stars."

"What sort of things?" I asked.

"Anyhow, she must have taught me pretty well," Sophy parried, "to be able to stand up to a psychologist when I wasn't quite four. Oh, she taught me about cats, how to stroke them and other animals, including people." She gave me a mischievous grin. "She taught me how space and time didn't mean anything. And she taught me how to keep cool and never to back down in the real clutches and how to—" she hesitated an instant—"love."

Her eyes were directed at me and her gaze was sinking deeper and deeper into mine as she said that last word. There wasn't the least thing trite or saccharine about it the way she said it. The way her gaze pierced me, I felt I was being possessed. Totally. I was afraid. Of course all this was a moment's fantasy.

"And she taught me love is forever and fierce," she finished, so softly it might have been ESP, or else more of my own fantasy, fortified by Norman Saylor's "guff" about the Anima.

But once again there came to me that odd sense of unidentifiable guilt, of something I'd buried very deep and still couldn't dig up—if it were wise to try.

Apparently Estelle hadn't noticed the interchange between Sophy and me, which was a happy wonder, as it would have provided fine ammunition for her theory of "Every female has a crush on you." Her wistful eyes looked through a wall.

"Excuse me, Sophy," she said, "but I'm afraid your mother was wrong about time." She ran a thin hand lightly across her graying hair. "We all grow old."

Sophy said, "But if it were that way, how could we ever wait long enough for the important things?" She added stoutly, "My mother told me to try to live at least a thousand years."

Estelle asked, not unkindly, "Did she tell you how?"

Sophy shook her head and quickly went on, for once a little brittlely, "My mother also left me some presents—"

Estelle glanced at the window and interrupted with "Well, whatever time means elsewhere, I'm afraid it's real here, or we have to act as if it were. It's getting late. It's been a nice party, but the Fosters will be getting worried. Andre, would you see Sophy home?"

One of the things Estelle always insists on, if it's after dark or merely the onset of twilight, is that I see any single woman home, be she a snooty fifty or a lissome eighteen, cleaning woman or scholar or life guard. I suppose it's a nice thing, really, a touch of the old courtesy—even when Estelle's mood changed and she berated me about the crush the lady had on me—and maybe I on her—when I got back from escort duty.

As soon as we got outside, Sophy and I saw it wasn't dark at all and that the sun or at least part of it was still above the horizon. So it seemed the most natural thing in the world for us to stroll hand in hand past the Fosters' down to the beach.

The Pacific was living up to her name. The tide was going out. We stood side by side on the wet, firm sand looking toward Japan. There was still a narrow, orange-yellow slice of sun above the distant water. There wasn't any spectacular sunset, just a low reddish glow in the west, because there wasn't a single cloud in the sky.

The sun went under. As usual I watched for the green flash some people can see under ideal atmospheric conditions at the instant the last sliver of sun vanishes. As usual, I didn't spot it. I explained about it to Sophy with a chuckle at my failure. She nodded.

And then it seemed the most natural thing in the world for us to stroll down the beach. At first we wandered separately, then once more hand in hand. Bright Venus winked on in the west, then golden Jupiter overhead, then icy-diamond Sirius, lower than Venus in the southeast, and somewhat above her the compact rectangle of yellow-red Betelgeuse and the other three big stars that are the chief ones of Orion, the Hunter.

Sophy said, "Andre, how would you like to go to the stars, just with me?"

"That'd be fun," I said, giving her hand a gentle squeeze.

"When we got to my planet," she said, "we could settle down and have cats. And babies."

Once again Norman's "guff" came to my mind. There was something eerie about the darkened beach now and perhaps about Sophy, too. I tried to make my grip on her hand light and neutral.

"You're a little young to be thinking about babies," I told her with a jocularity that didn't register in my voice. At the same time I was remembering that Anne of Austria had been betrothed to Louis XIII at eleven.

"Young and old mean different things different places," Sophy said. "Someone who's supposed to be a child on one planet may be a grownup on another."

Thinking of just Earth's many sharp intercultural differences, I couldn't but agree. I said, "Of course, Estelle would have to come along on the trip."

"No," Sophy said. "She doesn't like space. She'd never agree to it. And Mother told me you have to travel very light when you journey between stars. And besides—"

"You know, Sophie," I interrupted, "Estelle is a pretty sweet person, really, even if she's a little narrow-minded and vindictive."

Sophy said, "Yes, I liked playing high tea and other games with her. That's what makes it harder."

I went on quickly, "So I guess I'll just have to stay home on Earth and look after Estelle." My voice again failed to register the lightness and jocularity I intended.

"You're right, too, about Estelle needing to be looked after," Sophy agreed soberly. "I don't think she could make it even on Earth without you. So you'll just have to do something about her."

"And there isn't anything to do about her, so I'll just have to stay on Earth," I said, this time managing to register a tone of finality. I added gently, "A pity."

"It's more than a pity, Andre," Sophy said. "It's a tragedy. It's always a tragedy when true love is foiled."

That stopped me dead on the firm sand.

Sophy said, "A lot of people think kids can't know anything about tragedy. Andre, I've never told you or anyone the whole story about my Momma and Poppa. They were on an inspection-exploration ship checking up on Earth. They were on the team that came down. I wasn't born then, hadn't even been conceived—Momma told me all about it afterwards. They dug Earth, came to love it, and decided to stay, pretending to be Earth folk, until the next inspection ship came around. Permission was granted."

Sophy sighed in an infinitely world-weary way. "Things happened just as you'd expect. For a couple of years they scurried around and enjoyed themselves. Then they both got bored. People were so stupid and brutal here—even the nicest and sweetest of them, even Einstein and Gandhi, I guess, though I don't even see myself how that could be. And the next inspection ship might be five hundred years.

"Anyway, one night Poppa was away and Momma got so bored she went out to bars and got drunk and let an Earth man give her a baby. That was me."

A shiver went down my neck. I was still just standing. "Sophy," I asked, "did your mother have brown hair?"

I could not see Sophy's face, for it was long ago full dark, with only the tiny white breakers to see, and the feeble, low lights of Venice across the sand, and the stars above. But I could sense her eyes closed in thought, her faint frown.

"I don't know," she admitted at last. "Why can't I remember? But whatever the color was, there was a narrow silver streak running back from the middle of her forehead."

That did it for me. That was quite enough. I had found my hidden guilt. I suppose there are tens of thousands of women with such silver streaks in their hair. No matter. The mind recognizes logic, chance, and coincidence. But the feelings don't. For the feelings, the most improbable, airy possibility can be fully as real as a fact proven, witnessed, and sealed.

Because eleven years ago, you see, after six months of Lynn's last sickness, with Estelle tending her night and day as the child slowly and steadily weakened, and the doctors no help at all, and me spelling Estelle part of the nights and then going off to my editorial job in the mornings, I got fed up with it all. I took off one night and roamed the bars and forgot my troubles and felt my usual brilliant self, only more so. I met a beautiful babe, and bantered with her, and laid her—delicious!—and left her.

A beautiful babe with a silver streak down the middle of her hair. I didn't remember the color of the rest of it.

And then when I had got home, Lynn was dead. I don't think Estelle has ever forgiven me for being away that night. She never questioned me about it, but I think she guessed. It was then that life stopped meaning much for her.

Still motionless there on the beach, I grew chill as ice, although my heart was throbbing painfully. My hand went limp and Sophy's dropped out of it.

Why, Sophy might have been conceived the instant Lynn died.

My daughter's hand . . .

Sophy went on as if she hadn't noticed my reactions. "Momma didn't tell Poppa what had happened, but after a while he could see she was pregnant with me. They had terrible fights, mostly with words. Maybe being all alone in a strange world took away their control. After one bad quarrel, Poppa turned his gun on himself and vanished himself." She paused. "Momma told me all about it after I could understand a little of it. She thought I ought to know everything, good or bad. She planned that we'd wait for the next inspection ship, which might take less, very much less, than five hundred of your years, for our people have ways, which often work, of sensing if one of us is in distress on an alien planet. And then they re-route a ship for rescue if they reasonably can.

"But Momma let herself get too sad and too guilty about Poppa and me. She was the wisest woman in this world, but she couldn't save herself. I guess you can say she died of a broken heart."

I couldn't make any comment whatever, just go on standing there paralyzed.

"Well, anyhow," Sophy went on, suddenly brisk, *"there's* where we're going on our trip."

She had something of the Anima authority, all right. I followed her slim, ghostly finger to the center of Orion, where the belt and the sword now blazed, the whole of the constellation bespangled with tinier stars—the gaudiest and most gorgeous sight in the entire sky.

Then I realized for the first time it was pitch-dark, and through all my infinitely more serious wondering and fears, there stabbed the trivial but sharp concern that Sophy and I were out 'way after hours and God knows what the Fosters and Estelle would be thinking or doing.

Sophy found my hand and gripped it reassuringly. "Don't worry, Andre," she said. "Don't worry about the Fosters or Estelle. Things will work out. And especially don't worry about you and me, and how we feel toward each other. On my planet it's perfectly all right for a daughter and widowed father to marry, if they both want to."

For me, that was another dose of paralysis, though I'll always remember the feel of Sophy's slim little hand around mine.

I don't know how long that moment lasted. But before I could do anything, Sophy had let go of my hand to point once more at Orion and say in a voice closer to excitement than I'd ever heard it, "The sign! *They*'ve sent a ship for us. Hurry. *They* may be here tomorrow. We've got to get ready."

Then the faint scuff of her light, running feet across the dry sand.

I want to be very careful what I put down now, especially since I can't be sure whether what I saw, or thought I saw, came before what Sophy said, or afterwards, or somewhere during.

I looked up at Orion, and in the sword was a bright scarlet asterisk, consisting of eight narrow, straight lines radiating from the center, the whole appearance occupying about the diameter of the moon.

It instantly vanished.

Then I was running after Sophy, as usual making hard work in the dry sand.

I caught up with her finally in our street. We didn't talk about what had happened. I didn't have the breath to do so.

Lights were on in the Fosters' home and mine and both front doors stood open. But there were voices coming from mine. We headed toward it. I was gritting my teeth in cringing anticipation. I don't know about Sophy.

It could hardly have been worse. Estelle was playing it cool, leaning back in an armchair, and puffing a cigarette in her best eyebrow-raised, lady-of-the-manor style.

The two Fosters, whom I now saw for the first time, were pacing about everywhere. Or maybe stumbling and tottering would be better words. He was a senile hulk of a man, looking like a big upright log that had been bleaching on the beach for ten years. She was a scrunched-over little buzzard of a woman, forever darting her shiny black eyes around and backing most of her husband's imbecile plays. They both landed on me at once.

"What the hell were you doing, mister, out until all hours with Sophy?" the Hulk demanded.

"Yes, mister, what were you doing out with a little girl hours after dark?" the Buzzard supplemented.

I noticed that after one look at Sophy neither of the Fosters gave her another glance, or said a word to her, or laid a hand on her in love or anger. She stepped between them, took a place a yard behind them, and stood there as cool and unconcerned as I'd ever seen her.

"I was—" I began impatiently, and then hesitated.

Estelle cut in neatly, in a voice both imperious and plaintive, "Andre, these two crude persons pushed their way in. I would have sent for the police to put them out, except police are crude, too. Do something about them."

The Hulk blustered, "Mister, I'd have sent for the police long ago myself except out of consideration for your missus. Now I think I ought to ask them to haul her in, too."

The Buzzard bravely seconded, "Haul in the both of you. I'll have you know, we get *paid* for taking care of Sophy. Money from the Home and from the County, too."

"Shut up about that, Myra," the Hulk said.

Estelle remarked airly and speculatively, "Support money from two sources, eh? Is each aware of the other? I wonder how that would sound in court. Or your vile accusations against a distinguished author, even if you are playing footsie with some of the cruder members of the local Cossack post."

The Hulk said something unprintable, or rather (these days) not worth printing, about how writers and other hippies were darkening the skies of Los Angeles (apparently industrial fumes and automobile exhausts had nothing to do with it) and ought to be all shipped back to the Bronx, or Poland, or San Francisco, or somewhere.

As usual in a crisis, I'd said nothing much.

Quite an evening.

After a while the Hulk and the Buzzard went stumbling off, still complaining and breathing threats and warnings, with Sophy stepping lightly two paces in the rear. I wasn't a bit worried about anything they might do to her. She obviously had the good old Anima whiphand of them.

But I *was* worried about a lot of other things—things which of course I couldn't even hint of to Estelle. For a wonder she didn't nag me about "Sophy's crush," just kidded me a bit about the perils of taking nymphets for walks after dark and the astonishing degree to which most older Americans and married couples worried about the molestation of their darling daughters by middle-aged men, even if the latter were the most trusted of old friends.

Still, I had to take three pills to get to sleep.

Despite the pills, the reflex of habit woke me at dawn. Estelle was sleeping like a log. Nonetheless, I was very slow and cautious about slipping from between the sheets. The springs didn't creak. I sat on the edge of the bed and wormed my feet into thick woolen socks with thin, pliant leather soles stitched to them. Venice mornings are chilly.

Then I picked up my bathrobe and edged my way to the kitchen without knocking anything over. I started heating a half pot of stale coffee, then put on my thick robe over my pajamas. As soon as the coffee was barely hot, I downed a cup of it with a shudder and a grimace, heated the rest hotter, and bore a steaming cup of it to my icy, stern typewriter, lit my first cigarette, and sat down and stared at the cryptic, silent, loveless keyboard.

My mind was still quite muzzy with the three barbiturates I'd had. There wasn't a consequential thought in it, for which I was grateful.

My trance lasted five seconds or fifteen minutes, I don't know how long, when I thought I heard the faintest of scuffs, turned my head, and saw Sophy crossing the living room without seeing me. She was dressed exactly as when I'd first met her, except that now she held her little black plastic pistol in her hand. She vanished into the bedroom.

Drugged or not, I was up and after her like a silent flash.

All I remember glimpsing by the way was Selim backed up against the far wall. His fur was bristled out as much as when the dog had chased him. Only now his eyes weren't furious, but terrified.

I saw into the bedroom. Sophy was leaning grave-faced over the bed and had the muzzle of the plastic pistol an inch from Estelle's temple.

All I could remember was how there had been a click and the big dog had been gone.

I hurled myself silently forward so I landed half on the bed. My hand closed around Sophy's hand and the plastic pistol and reversed the aim of the latter.

There was a click.

Then Sophy wasn't there at all, and I was just holding the black plastic pistol, which was so tiny my big hand concealed it completely, and Estelle had reared up from the fleshy-scented warm sheets. Face puffed with sleep, hair stringy as Medusa's, eyes blazing with the fierceness of a fury's (or an Anima's?), she was yelling, "What do you mean waking me up like this? Have you finally gone crazy like I've always told you you would?"

Later that day I hid the little toylike pistol where I thought no one would ever find it.

Estelle and I had a little trouble over Sophy, but really not much. The Fosters came over and gave us another hard time. Then the local police dropped in and asked some questions, but Estelle was on her good behavior and they didn't seem very interested. I guessed the Fosters had set them on and they didn't think much of the Fosters. Paranoids, especially elderly ones, can be a bore to the police.

And a languid young man came over from the Home for the Wanted and most politely asked us a few questions and took a few notes and thanked us courteously and went his languid way. We said a couple of nice things about Abbott Kinney, but I don't think he'd ever heard of the man.

Next morning I looked for the gun—or "toy"—where I'd hidden it. It was gone.

Maybe *they*—the Ones of the Red Sign—tracked it down and took it away with them, off this planet.

At least I hope so. I would hate to think of it falling into the hands of any Earth child—or any Earth adult, for that matter.

And sometimes I hope it "disappeared" Sophy back to her own planet. But from the way she talked about what happened to Poppa, I very much doubt that.

In the midst of Life we are in Death.

Yet in the midst of Death we are in Life.

THE GREAT SUPERSONIC ZEPPELIN RACE
Ben Bova

"You can make a supersonic aircraft that doesn't produce a sonic boom," said Bob Wisdom.

For an instant the whole cafeteria seemed to go quiet. Bob was sitting at a table by the big picture window that overlooked Everett Aircraft Co.'s parking lot. It was drizzling out there, as it usually did in the spring. Through the haze, Mt. Olympia's snow-topped peak could barely be seen.

Bob smiled quizzically at his lunch pals. He was tall and lanky, round-faced in a handsome sort of way, with dark thinning hair and dark eyes that were never somber, even in the midst of Everett Aircraft's worst layoffs and cutbacks.

"A supersonic aircraft," mumbled Ray Kurtz from inside his beard.

"With no sonic boom," added Tommy Rohr.

Bob Wisdom smiled and nodded.

"What's the catch?" asked Richard Grand in a slightly Anglified accent.

The cafeteria resumed its clattering, chattering noises. The drizzle outside continued to soak the few scraggly trees and pitiful shrubs planted around the half-empty parking lot.

"Catch?" Bob echoed, trying to look hurt. "Why should there be a catch?"

"Because if someone could build a supersonic aircraft that

119

doesn't shatter people's eardrums, obviously someone would be doing it," Grand answered.

"We could do it," Bob agreed pleasantly, "but we're not."

"Why not?" Kurtz asked.

Bob shrugged elaborately.

Rohr waggled a finger at Bob. "There's something going on in that aerodynamicist's head of yours. This is a gag, isn't it?"

"No gag," Bob replied innocently. "I'm surprised that nobody's thought of the idea before."

"What's the go of it?" Grand asked. He had just read a biography of James Clerk Maxwell and was trying to sound English, despite the fact that Maxwell was a Scot.

"Well," Bob said, with a bigger grin than before, "there's a type of wing that the German aerodynamicist Adolph Busemann invented. Instead of making the wings flat, though, you build your supersonic aircraft with a ringwing . . ."

"Ringwing?"

"Sure." Leaning forward and propping one elbow on the cafeteria table, Bob pulled a felt-tip pen from his shirt pocket and sketched on the paper placemat.

"See? Here's the fuselage of a supersonic plane." He drew a narrow cigar shape. "Now we wrap the wing around it, like a sleeve. It's actually two wings, one inside the other, and all the shock waves that cause the sonic boom get trapped inside the wings and get canceled out. No sonic boom."

Grand stared at the sketch, then looked up at Bob, then stared at the sketch some more. Rohr looked expectant, waiting for the punch line. Kurtz frowned, looking like a cross between Abe Lincoln and Karl Marx.

"I don't know much about aerodynamics," Rohr said

slowly, "but that is a sort of Busemann biplane you're talking about, isn't it?"

Bob nodded.

"Ahah . . . and isn't it true that the wings of a Busemann biplane produce no lift?"

"Right," Bob admitted.

"No lift?" Kurtz snapped. "Then how the hell do you get it off the ground?"

Trying to look completely serious, Bob answered, "You can't get it off the ground if it's an ordinary airplane. It's got to be lighter-than-air. You fill the central body with helium."

"A zeppelin?" Kurtz squeaked.

Rohr started laughing. "You sonofabitch. You had us all going there for a minute."

Grand said, "Interesting."

John Driver sat behind a cloud of blue smoke that he puffed from a reeking pipe. His office always smelled like an opium den gone sour. His secretary, a luscious and sweet-tempered girl of Greek-Italian ancestry, had worn out eight strings of rosary beads in the vain hope that he might give up smoking.

"A supersonic zeppelin?" Driver snapped angrily. "Ridiculous!"

Squinting into the haze in an effort to find his boss, Grand answered, "Don't be too hasty to dismiss the concept. It might have some merit. At the very least, I believe we could talk NASA or the Transportation people into giving us money to investigate the idea."

At the sound of the word "money," Driver took the pipe out of his teeth and waved some of the smoke away. He peered at Grand through reddened eyes. Driver was lean-faced, with hard features and a gaze that he liked to think was piercing. His jaw was slightly overdeveloped from biting through so many pipe stems.

"You have to spend money to make money in this business," Driver said in his most penetrating *Fortune* magazine acumen.

"I realize that," Grand answered stiffly. "But I'm quite willing to put my own time into this. I really believe we may be onto something that can save our jobs."

Driver drummed his slide-rule-calloused fingertips on his desktop. "All right," he said at last. "Do it on your own time. When you've got something worth showing, come to me with it. Not anyone else, you understand. Me."

"Right, Chief." Whenever Grand wanted to flatter Driver, he called him "Chief."

After Grand left his office, Driver sat at his desk for a long, silent while. The company's business had been going to hell over the past few years. There was practically no market for high-technology work any more. The military were more interested in sandbags than supersonic planes. NASA was wrapping tourniquets everywhere in an effort to keep from bleeding to death. The newly reorganized Department of Transportation and Urban Renewal hardly understood what a Bunsen burner was.

"A supersonic zeppelin," Driver muttered to himself. It sounded ridiculous. But then, so did air cushion vehicles and Wankel engines. Yet companies were making millions on those ideas.

"A supersonic zeppelin," he repeated. "SSZ."

Then he noticed that his pipe had gone out. He reached into his left-top desk drawer for a huge blue-tipped kitchen match and started puffing the pipe alight again. Great clouds of smoke billowed upward as he said:

"SSZ . . . no sonic boom . . . might not even cause air pollution."

Driver climbed out of the cab, clamped his pipe in his teeth, and gazed up at the magnificent glass and stainless steel façade of the new office building that housed the Transportation and Urban Renewal Department.

"So this is TURD headquarters," he muttered.

"This is it," replied Tracy Keene, who had just paid off the cabbie and come up to stand beside Driver. Keene was Everett Aircraft's crackerjack Washington representative, a large, round man who always conveyed the impression that he knew things nobody else knew. Keene's job was to find new customers for Everett, placate old customers when Everett inevitably alienated them, and pay off taxicabs. The job involved grotesque amounts of wining and dining, and Keene—who had once been as wiry and agile as a weak-hitting shortstop— seemed to grow larger and rounder every time Driver came to Washington. But what he was gaining in girth he was losing in hair, Driver noticed.

"Let's go," Keene said. "We don't want to be late." He lumbered up the steps to the magnificent glass doors of the magnificent new building.

The building was in Virginia, not the District of Columbia. Like all new Government agencies, it was headquartered outside the city proper. The fact that one of this agency's major responsibilities was to find ways to revitalize the major cities and stop urban sprawl somehow never entered into consideration when the site for its location was chosen.

Two hours later, Keene was half-dozing in a straight-backed metal chair and Driver was taking the last of an eight-inch-thick pile of viewgraph slides off the projector. The projector fan droned hypnotically in the darkened room. They were in the office of Roger K. Memo, Assistant Under Director for Transportation Research of TURD.

Memo and his chief scientific advisor, Dr. Alonzo Pencilbeam, were sitting on one side of the small table. Keene was resting peacefully on the other side. Driver stood up at the head of the table, frowning beside the viewgraph projector. The only light in the room came from the projector, which now threw a blank glare onto the wan yellow wall that served in place of a screen. Smoke from Driver's pipe sifted through the cone of light.

Driver snapped the projector off. The light and the fan's whirring noise abruptly stopped. Keene jerked fully awake and, without a word, reached up and flicked the wall switch that turned on the overhead lights.

Although the magnificent building was sparkling new, Memo's office somehow looked instant-seedy. There wasn't enough furniture in it for its size: only an ordinary steel desk and swivel chair, a half-empty bookcase, and this little conference table with four chairs that didn't match. The walls and floor were bare, and there was a distinct echo when anyone spoke or even walked across the room. The only window had vertical slats instead of a curtain, and it looked out on an automobile graveyard. The only decoration on the walls was a diploma, Memo's doctorate degree, bought from an obscure Mohawk Valley college for $200 without the need to attend classes.

Driver stood by the projector, frowning through his own smoke.

"Well, what do you think?" he asked subtly.

Memo pursed his lips. He was jowly fat, completely bald,

wore glasses and rumpled gray suits.

"I don't know," he said firmly. "It sounds . . . unusual . . ."

Dr. Pencilbeam was sitting back in his chair and smiling beatifically. His Ph.D. had been earned during the 1930's, when he had to work nights and weekends to stay alive and in school. He was still very thin, fragile-looking, with the long skinny limbs of a praying mantis.

Pencilbeam dug in his jacket pockets and pulled out a pouch of tobacco and cigarette paper. "It certainly looks interesting," he said in a soft voice. "I think it's technically feasible . . . and lots of fun."

Memo snorted. "We're not here to enjoy ourselves."

Keene leaned across the table and fixed Memo with his best here's-something-from-behind-the-scenes look:

"Do you realize how the Administration would react to a sensible program for a supersonic aircraft? With the *Concorde* going broke and the Russian SST grounded . . . you could put this country out in front again."

"H'mm," said Memo. "But . . ."

"Balance of payments," Keene intoned knowingly. "Gold outflow . . . aerospace employment . . . national prestige . . . the President would be awfully impressed.

"H'mm," Memo repeated. "I see . . .."

The cocktail party was in full swing. It was nearly impossible to hear your own voice in the swirling babble of chatter and clinking glassware. In the middle of the sumptuous living room, the Vice President was demonstrating his golf swing. Out in the foyer, three Senators were comparing fact-finding tours they were arranging for the Riviera, Rio de Janeiro, and American Samoa, respectively. The Cabinet wives held sway in the glittering dining room.

Roger K. Memo never drank anything stronger than ginger ale. He stood in the doorway between the living room and foyer, lip reading the Senators' conversation about travel plans. When the trio broke up and Senator Goodyear (R., Ohio) headed back toward the bar, Memo intercepted him.

"Hello, Senator!" Memo shouted heartily. It was the only way to be heard over the party noise.

"Ah . . . hello." Senator Goodyear obviously knew that he knew Memo, but just as obviously couldn't recall his name, rank, or influence rating.

Goodyear was nearly six feet tall, and towered over Memo's paunchy figure. Together they shouldered their way through the crowd around the bar. Goodyear ordered bourbon on the rocks, and therefore so did Memo. But he merely held onto his glass, while the Senator immediately began to gulp at his drink.

A statuesque blonde in a spectacular gown sauntered past them. The Senator's eyes tracked her like a range finder following a target.

"I hear you're going to Samoa," Memo shouted as they edged away from the bar, following the girl.

"Eh . . . yes," Goodyear answered cautiously, a tone he usually employed with newspaper reporters.

"Beautiful part of the world," Memo yelled.

The blonde slipped an arm around the waist of a young, long-haired man and they disappeared into another room together. Goodyear turned his attention back to his drink.

"I said," Memo repeated, standing on tiptoes, "that Samoa is a beautiful part of the world."

Nodding, Goodyear said, "I'm going to investigate the ecological conditions there . . . my committee is considering legislation on ecology."

"Of course, of course. You've got to see things first-hand if you're going to enact meaningful laws."

Slightly less guardedly, Goodyear said, "Exactly."

"It's such a long way off, though," Memo said. "It must take considerable thought to decide to make such a long trip."

"Well . . . you know we can't think of our own comforts when we're in public service."

"Yes, of course. . . . Will you be taking the SST? I understand QUANTAS flies it out of San Francisco . . ."

Suddenly alert again, Goodyear snapped, "Never! I always fly American planes on American airlines."

"Very patriotic," Memo applauded. "And sensible, too. Those Aussies don't know how to run an airline. And any plane made by the British *and* the French . . . well, I don't know. I understand it's financially in trouble."

Goodyear nodded again. "That's what I hear."

"Still—it's a shame that the United States doesn't have a supersonic aircraft. It would cut your travel time in half. Give you twice as much time to stay in Samoa . . . investigating."

The hearing room in the Capitol was jammed with reporters and cameramen. Senator Goodyear sat in the center of the long front table, as befits the committee chairman.

All through the hot summer morning the committee had listened to witnesses: John Driver, Roger K. Memo, Alonzo Pencilbeam, and many others. The concept of the supersonic zeppelin unfolded before the newsmen, and started to take on definite solidity right there in the rococo-trimmed hearing room.

Senator Goodyear sat there solemnly all morning, listening to the carefully rehearsed testimony, watching the greenery outside the big sunny window. Whenever he thought about the TV cameras, he sat up straighter and tried to look lean and tough, like Gary Cooper. Goodyear had a drawer full of Gary Cooper movies on video cassettes in his Ohio home.

Now it was his turn to summarize what the witnesses had said. He looked straight at the nearest camera, trying to come across strong and sympathetic, like the sheriff in *High Noon.*

"Gentlemen," he began, immediately antagonizing the eighteen women in the audience, "I believe that what we have heard here today can mark the beginning of a new program that will revitalize the aerospace industry and put America back in the forefront of international commerce . . ."

One of the younger Senators at the far end of the table interrupted:

"Excuse me, Mr. Chairman, but my earlier question about pollution was never answered. Won't the SSZ use the same kinds of jet engines that the SST was going to use? And won't they cause just as much pollution?"

Goodyear glowered at the junior member's impudence, but controlled his temper well enough to say only, "Em . . . Dr. Pencilbeam, would you care to answer that question?"

Pencilbeam, seated at one of the witness tables, looked startled for a moment. Then he hunched his bony frame around the microphone in front of him and said:

"The pollution arguments about the SST were never substantiated. There were wild claims that if you operated jet engines up in the high stratosphere, you would eventually cause a permanent cloud layer over the whole Earth or destroy the ozone up there and thus let in enough solar ultraviolet radiation to cause millions of cancer deaths. But these claims were never proved."

"But it was never disproved, either, was it?" the junior Senator said.

Before Pencilbeam could respond, Senator Goodyear grabbed his own microphone and nearly shouted, "Rest assured that we are all well aware of the possible pollution problems. At the moment, though, there is no problem because there is no SSZ. Our aerospace industry is suffering, employment is 'way down, and the whole economy is in a bad way. The SSZ project will provide jobs and boost the economy. As part of the project, we will consult with the English and French and see what their pollution problems are—if any. And our own American engineers will, I assure you, find ways to eliminate any and all pollution coming from the SSZ engines."

Looking rather disturbed, Pencilbeam started to add something to Goodyear's statement. But Memo put a hand over the scientist's microphone and shook his head in a strong negative.

Mark Sequoia was hiking along a woodland trail in Fairmont Park, Philadelphia, when the news reached him.

Once a flaming crusader for ecological salvation and against pollution, Sequoia had made the mistake of letting the Commonwealth of Pennsylvania hire him as the state ecology director. He had spent the past five years earnestly and honestly trying to clean up Pennsylvania, a job that had driven four generations of the original Penn family into early graves. The deeper Sequoia buried himself in the solid wastes and politics of Pittsburgh, Philadelphia, Chester, Erie, and other hopeless cities, the fewer followers and national headlines he attracted.

Now he led a scraggly handful of sullen high school students through the soot-ravaged woodlands of Fairmont Park on a steaming July afternoon, picking up empty beer cans and loaded prophylactics—and keeping a wary eye out for muggers. Even full daylight was no protection against assault. And the school kids with him wouldn't help. Half of them would jump in and join the fun.

Sequoia was broad-shouldered, almost burly. His face had been seamed by weather and press conferences. He looked strong and fit, but lately his back had been giving him trouble, and his old trick knee . . .

He heard someone pounding up the trail behind him.

"Mark! Mark!"

Sequoia turned to see Larry Helper, his last and therefore most trusted aide, running along the gravel path toward him, waving a copy of the *Evening Bulletin* over his head. Newspaper pages were slipping from his sweaty grasp and fluttering off across the grass.

"Littering," Sequoia mumbled in the tone sometimes used by bishops when faced with a case of heresy.

"Some of you men," Sequoia said in his best Lone Ranger voice, "pick up those newspaper pages."

A couple of kids lackadaisically ambled after the fluttering sheets.

"Mark, look here!" Helper skidded to a stop and breathlessly waved the front page of the newspaper. "Look!"

Sequoia grabbed his aide's wrist and took the newspaper from him. He frowned at Helper, he cringed and stepped back.

"I . . . I thought you'd want to see . . ."

Satisfied that he was in control of things, Sequoia turned his attention to the front page headline.

"Supersonic *zeppelin?*"

By nightfall, Sequoia was meeting with a half-dozen men and women in the basement of a prosperous downtown church that specialized in worthy causes capable of filling the pews upstairs.

Sequoia was pacing across the little room in which they were meeting. There was no table, just a few folding chairs scattered around, and a locked bookcase stuffed with books on sex and marriage.

"No, we've got to do something dramatic!" Sequoia pounded a fist into his open palm. "We can't just drive down to Washington and call a press conference . . ."

"Automobiles pollute," said one of the women, a comely redhead, whose eyes never left Sequoia's broad, sturdy-looking figure.

"We could take the train; it's electrical."

"Power stations pollute."

"Airplanes pollute, too."

"What about riding down on horseback? Like Paul Revere!"

"Horses pollute."

"They do?"

"Ever been around a stable?"

"Oh."

Sequoia pounded his fist again. "I've got it!" His hand stung; he had hit it too hard.

"What?"

"A balloon! We'll ride down to Washington in a nonpolluting, helium-filled balloon. That's the dramatic way to emphasize our point!"

"Fantastic!"

"Marvelous!"

The redhead was panting with excitement. "Oh, Mark, you're so clever. So dedicated." There were tears in her eyes.

Helper said softly, "Uh . . . does anybody know where we

can get a balloon? And how much they cost?"

Sequoia glared at him.

When the meeting finally broke up, Helper had the task of finding a suitable balloon, preferably for free. Sequoia would spearhead the effort to raise money for a knockdown fight against the SSZ. The redhead volunteered to assist him. They left arm in arm.

The auditorium in Foggy Bottom was crammed with newsmen. TV lights were glaring at the empty podium. The reporters and cameramen shuffled, coughed, talked to each other. Then:

"Ladies and gentlemen, the President of the United States."

They all stood up and applauded politely as the President strode across the stage toward the podium in his usual bunched-together, shoulder-first football style. His dark face was somber under its beetling brows.

The President gripped the podium and nodded, with a perfunctory smile, to a few of his favorites. The newsmen sat down. The cameras started rolling.

"I have a statement to make about the tragic misfortune that has overtaken one of our finest public figures—Mark Sequoia. According to the latest report I have received from the Coast Guard—no more than ten minutes ago—there is still no trace of him or his party. Apparently the balloon they were riding in was blown out to sea two days ago, and nothing has been heard from them since.

"Now let me make this perfectly clear. Mr. Sequoia was frequently on the other side of the political fence from me, your President. He was often a critic of my policies and actions, the policies and actions of your President. He was on his way to

Washington to protest our new SSZ project when this unfortunate accident occurred—to protest the SSZ project despite the fact that it will employ thousands of aerospace engineers who are otherwise unemployable and untrainable. Despite the fact that it will save the American dollar on the international market and salvage American prestige in the technological battleground of the world.

"Now, in spite of the fact that some of us—such as our Vice President, as is well known—feel that Mr. Sequoia carried the Constitutional guarantee of free speech a bit too far, despite all this, mind you, I—as your President and Commander-in-Chief—have dispatched every available military, Coast Guard, and Boy Scout plane, ship, and foot patrol to search the entire coastline and coastal waters between Philadelphia and Washington. We will find Mark Sequoia and his brave party of misguided ecology nuts . . . or their remains.

"Are there any questions?"

The Associated Press reporter, a hickory-tough old man with huge, thick glasses and a white goatee, stood up and asked in stentorian tones:

"Is it true that Sequoia's balloon was blown off course by a flight of Air Force fighter planes that buzzed it?"

The President made a smile that looked somewhat like a grimace and said:

"I'm glad you asked that question . . ."

Ronald Eames Trafalgar was Her Majesty's Ambassador Plenipotentiary to the Government of the Union of Soviet Socialist Republics.

He sat rather uneasily in the rear seat of the Bentley, watching the white-boled birch trees flash past the car windows. The first snow of autumn was already on the ground, the trees were almost entirely bare, the sky was a pewter gray. Trafalgar shivered with the iron cold of the steppes, even inside his heavy woolen coat.

Next to him sat Sergei Mihailovitch Traktor, Minister of Technology. The two men were old friends, despite their vast differences in outlook, upbringing, and appearance. Trafalgar could have posed for Horatio Hornblower illustrations: he was tall, slim, poised, just a touch of gray at his well-brushed temples. Traktor looked like an automobile mechanic (which he once was): stubby, heavy-faced, shifty eyes.

"I can assure you that this car is absolutely clean," Trafalgar said calmly, still watching the melancholy birch forest sliding by. The afternoon sun was an indistinct bright blur behind the trees, trying to burn its way through the gray overcast.

"And let me assure you," Traktor said in flawless English, a startling octave higher than the Englishman's voice, "that *all* your cars are bugged."

Trafalgar laughed lightly. "Dear man. We constantly find your bugs and plant them next to tape recordings of the Beatles."

"You only find the bugs we want you to find."

"Nonsense."

"Truth." Traktor didn't mention the eleven kilos of electronic gear that had been strapped to various parts of his fleshy anatomy before he had been allowed to visit the British embassy.

"Ah, well, no matter . . ." Trafalgar gave up the argument with an airy wave of his hand. "The basic question is quite simple: what are you going to do about this ridiculous supersonic zeppelin idea of the Americans?"

Traktor pursed his lips and studied his friend's face for a moment, like a garage mechanic trying to figure out how much a customer will hold still for.

"Why do you call it ridiculous?" he asked.

"You don't think it's ridiculous?" Trafalgar asked back.

They sparred for more than an hour before they both finally admitted that (a) their own supersonic transport planes were financially ruinous; and (b) they were both secretly working on plans to build supersonic zeppelins.

After establishing that confidence, both men were silent for a long, long time. The car drove out to the limit allowed for a British embassy vehicle by diplomatic protocol, then headed back for Moscow. The driver could clearly see the onion-shaped spires of churches before Trafalgar finally broke down and asked quietly:

"Em . . . Sergei, old man . . . do you suppose that we could work together on this zeppelin thing? It might save us both a good deal of money and time. And it would help us to catch up with the Americans."

"Impossible," said Traktor.

"I'm sure the thought has crossed your mind before this," Trafalgar said.

"Working with a capitalist nation . . ."

"Two capitalist nations," Trafalgar corrected. "The French are in with us."

Traktor said nothing.

"After all, you've worked with the French before. It's . . . difficult, I know. But it can be done. And my own Government is now in the hands of the Socialist Party."

"Improbable," said Traktor.

"And you *do* want to overtake the Americans, don't you?"

The President's desk was cleared of papers. Nothing cluttered the broad expanse of redwood except three phones (red, white, and black), a memento from an early Latin America tour (a fist-sized rock), and a ping-pong paddle.

The President sat back in the elevated chair behind the desk and fired instructions at his personal staff.

"I want to make it absolutely clear," he was saying to his press secretary, "that we are not in a race with the Russians or anybody else. We're building our SSZ for very sound economic and social reasons, not for competition with the Russians."

"Right, Chief," said the press secretary.

He turned to his top Congressional liaison man. "And you'd better make darned certain that the Senate Appropriations Committee votes the extra funds for the SSZ. Tell them that if we don't get the extra funding, we'll fall behind the Reds.

"And I want you," he said to the Director of TURD, "to spend every nickel of your existing SSZ money as fast as you can. Otherwise we won't be able to get Congress to put in more money."

"Yessir."

"But, Chief," the head of Budget Management started to object.

"I know what you're going to say," the President said to the top BUM. "I'm perfectly aware that money doesn't grow on trees. But we've got to make the SSZ a success . . . and before next November. Take money from education, from poverty, from the space program—anything. I want that SSZ flying by next spring, when I'm scheduled to visit Paris, Moscow, and Peking."

The whole staff gasped in sudden realization of the President's master plan.

"That's entirely correct," he said, smiling slyly at them. "I want to be the first Chief of State to cross the Atlantic, Europe, and Asia in a supersonic aircraft."

The VA hospital in Hagerstown had never seen so many reporters. There were reporters in the lobby, reporters lounging in the halls, reporters bribing nurses, reporters sneaking into elevators and surgical theaters (where they inevitably fainted). The parking lot was a jumble of cars bearing press stickers.

Only two reporters were allowed to see Mark Sequoia on any given day, and they had to share their story with all the other newsmen. Today the two—picked by lot—were a crusty old veteran from UPI and a rather pretty blonde from *Women's Wear Daily.*

"But I've told your colleagues what happened at least a dozen times," Sequoia mumbled from behind a swathing of bandages.

He was hanging by both arms and legs from four traction braces, his backside barely touching the bed. Bandages covered 80 percent of his body.

The two reporters stood by his bed. UPI looked flinty as he scribbled some notes on a rumpled sheet of paper. The blonde had a tiny tape recorder in her hand.

She looked misty-eyed. "Are . . . are you in much pain?"

"Not really," Sequoia answered bravely, with a slight tremor in his voice.

"Why the damned traction?" UPI asked in a tone reminiscent of a cement mixer riding over a gravel road. "The docs said there weren't any broken bones."

"Splinters," Sequoia said weakly.

"Bone splinters? Oh, how awful!" gasped the blonde.

"No—" Sequoia corrected. "Splinters. When the balloon came down, it landed in a clump of trees just outside of Hagerstown. We all suffered from thousands of splinters. It took the surgical staff here three days to pick all the splinters out of us. The chief of surgery said he was going to save the wood and build a scale model of the *Titanic* with it. . . ."

"Oh, how painful!" The blonde insisted on gasping. She gasped very well, Sequoia noted, watching her blouse.

"And what about your hair?" asked UPI gruffly.

Sequoia felt himself blush. "I . . . I must have been very frightened. After all, we were aloft in an open balloon for six days, without food, without anything to drink except a sixpack of beer that one of my aides brought along. We went through a dozen different thunderstorms . . ."

"With lightning?" the blonde asked.

Nodding painfully, Sequoia added, "We all thought we were going to die."

UPI frowned. "So your hair turned white from fright. There was some talk that cosmic rays might have done it."

"Cosmic rays? We weren't that high . . . Cosmic rays don't have any effect until you get to very high altitude . . . isn't that right?"

"How high did you go?"

"I don't know," Sequoia answered. "We didn't have an altimeter with us. Those thunderstorms pushed us pretty high, the air got kind of thin . . ."

"But not high enough for cosmic ray damage."

"I doubt it."

"Too bad," said UPI. "Would've made a better story than just being scared. Hair turned white by cosmic rays. Maybe even sterilized."

"Sterilized?"

"Cosmic rays do that, too," UPI said. "I checked."

"Well, we weren't that high."

"You're sure?"

"Ye . . . well, I don't think we were that high."

"But you could have been."

Shrugging was sheer torture, Sequoia found out.

"Okay, but those thunderstorms could've lifted you pretty damned high . . ."

The door opened and a horse-faced nurse said firmly, "That's all, please. Mr. Sequoia must rest now."

"Okay, I think I got something to hang a story onto," UPI said with a happy grin on his seamed face.

The blonde looked shocked and terribly upset. "You . . . you don't think you were really sterilized, do you?"

Sequoia tried to make himself sound worried and brave at the same time. "I don't know. I just . . . don't know."

Late that night the blonde snuck back into his room. If she knew the difference between sterilization and impotence, she didn't tell Sequoia about it. On his part, he forgot about his still-tender skin and his traction braces. The day nurse found him the next morning, unconscious, one shoulder dislocated, his skin terribly inflamed, most of his bandages rubbed off, and a silly grin on his face.

"Will you look at this!"

Senator Goodyear tossed the morning *Post* across the breakfast table to his wife. She was a handsome woman: nearly as tall as her husband, athletically lean, shoulder-length dark hair with just a wisp of silver. She always dressed for breakfast just as carefully as for dinner. This morning she was going riding, so she wore slacks and a turtle-neck sweater that outlined her figure.

But the Senator was more interested in the *Post* article. "That Sequoia! He'll stop at nothing to destroy me! Just because the Ohio River melted his houseboat once, years ago . . . he's been out to crucify me ever since."

Mrs. Goodyear looked up from the newspaper. "Sterilized? You mean that people who fly in the SSZ could be sterilized by cosmic rays?"

"Utter nonsense!" Goodyear snapped.

"Of course," his wife murmured soothingly.

But after the Senator drove off in his chauffeured limousine, Mrs. Goodyear made three phone calls. One was to the Smithsonian Institution. The second was to a friend in the Zero Population Growth movement. The third was to the underground Washington headquarters of the Women's International Terrorist Conspiracy from Hell. Unbeknownst to her husband or any of her friends or associates, Mrs. Goodyear was an undercover agent for WITCH.

The first snow of Virginia's winter was sifting gently past Roger K. Memo's office window. He was pacing across the plastic-tiled floor, his footsteps faintly echoing in the too-large room. Copies of the Washington *Post,* New York *Times,* and *Aviation Week* were spread across his desk.

Dr. Pencilbeam sat at one of the unmatched conference chairs, all bony limbs and elbows and knees.

"Relax, Roger," he said calmly. "Congress isn't going to stop the SSZ. It means too many jobs, too much international prestige. And besides, the President has staked his credibility on it."

"That's what worries me," Memo mumbled.

"What?"

But Memo's eye was caught by movement outside his window. He waddled past his desk and looked out at the street below.

"Oh, my God."

"What's going on?" Pencilbeam unfolded like a pocket ruler into a six-foot-long human and hurried to the window.

Outside, in the thin mushy snow, a line of somber men was filing down the street past the TURD building. Silently they bore screaming signs:

> STOP THE SSZ
> DON'T STERILIZE THE HUMAN RACE
> SSZ MURDERS UNBORN CHILDREN
> ZEPPELINS, GO HOME

"Isn't that one with the sign about unborn children a priest?" Pencilbeam asked.

Memo shrugged. "Your eyes are better than mine."

"Ah-hah! And look at this!"

Pencilbeam pointed further down the street. A swarm of women was advancing on the building. They also carried signs:

> SSZ FOR ZPG
> ZEPPELINS SI! BABIES NO
> ZEPPELINS FOR POPULATION CONTROL
> UP THE SSZ

Memo visibly sagged at the window. "This . . . this is awful . . ."

The women marched through the thin snowfall and straight into the line of picketing men. Instantly the silence was shattered by shouts and taunts. Shrill female voices battled against rumbling baritones and basses. Signs wavered. Bodies pushed. Someone screamed. One sign swung against a skull and then bloody war broke out.

Memo and Pencilbeam watched aghast until the helmeted tac squad police doused the whole scene with riot gas, clubbed men and women impartially, and dragged everyone off.

The huge factory assembly bay was filled with the skeleton of a giant dirigible. Great aluminum ribs stretched from titanium nosecap back toward the more intricate cagework of the tail fins. Tiny men with flashing laser welders crawled along the ribbing like maggots cleaning the bones of a noble whale.

Even the jet engines sitting on their loading pallets dwarfed human scale. Some of the welders held clandestine poker games inside them. John Driver and Richard Grand stood beside one of them, craning their necks to watch the welding work going on far overhead. The assembly bay rang to the shouts of working men, the hum of electrical machinery, and the occasional clatter of metal against metal.

"It's going to be some Christmas party if Congress cancels the project," Driver said gloomily from behind his inevitable pipe.

"Oh, they wouldn't dare cancel it, now that Women's Liberation is behind it," said Grand with a sardonic little smile.

Driver glared at him. "With those bitches for allies, you don't need any enemies. Half those idiots in Congress will vote against us just to prove that they're not scared of Women's Lib."

"Do you really think so?" Grand asked.

He always acts as if he knows more than I do, Driver thought. It had taken him several years to realize that Grand actually knew rather less than most people—but he had a way of hiding this behind protective language.

"Yes, I really think so!" Driver snapped. Then he pulled his pipe out of his mouth and jabbed it in the general direction of Grand's eyeballs. "And listen to me, kiddo. I've been working on that secretary of mine since the last goddamned Christmas party. If this project falls through and the party's a bust, that palpitating hunk of female flesh is going to run home and cry. And so will I!"

Grand blinked several times, then murmured, "Pity."

The banner saying HAPPY HOLIDAYS drooped sadly across one wall of the cafeteria. Outside in the darkness, lights glimmered, cars were moving, and a bright moon lit the snowy peak of Mt. Olympia.

But inside Everett Aircraft's cafeteria there was nothing but gloom. The Christmas party had been a dismal flop, especially so since half the company's employees had received their layoff notices the day before.

The tables had been pushed to one side of the cafeteria to make room for a dance floor. Syrupy music was oozing out of the loud-speakers in the acoustic-tile ceiling. But no one was dancing.

Bob Wisdom sat at one of the tables, propping his aching head on his hands. Ray Kurtz and Tommy Rohr sat with him, equally dejected.

"Why the hell did they have to cancel the project two days before Christmas?" Rohr asked rhetorically.

"Makes for more pathos," Kurtz muttered from inside his beard.

"It's pathetic, all right," Wisdom said. "I've never seen so many secretaries crying at once."

"Even Driver was crying," Rohr said.

"Well," Kurtz said, staring at his half-finished drink on the table before him, "Sequoia did it. He's a big national hero again."

"And we're on the bread line," Rohr said.

"You get laid off?"

"Not yet . . . but it's coming. This place will be closing its doors before another year is out."

"It's not that bad," said Wisdom. "There's still the Air Force work."

Rohr frowned. "You know what gets me? The way the whole project was scrapped, without giving us a chance to build one of the damned zeps and see how they work. Without a goddam chance!"

Kurtz said, "Congressmen are scared of being sterilized."

"Or castrated by Women's Lib."

"Next time you dream up a project, Bob, make it underground. Something in a lead mine. Then the Congressmen won't have to worry about cosmic rays."

Wisdom started to laugh, then held off. "You know," he said slowly, "you just might have something there."

"What?"

"Where?"

"A supersonic transport—in a tunnel."

"Oh, for Chri . . ."

Wisdom sat up straight in his chair. "No, listen. You could make an air cushion vehicle go supersonic. If you put it in a tunnel, you get away from the sonic boom and the pollution . . ."

"Hey, the safety aspects would be a lot better, too."

Kurtz shook his head. "You guys are crazy! Who the hell's going to dig tunnels all over the United States?"

But Wisdom waved him down. "Somebody will. Now, the way I see the design of this . . . SSST, I guess we call it."

"SSST?"

"Sure," he answered, grinning. "Supersonic subway train."

CUES
Gene Wolfe

"Cues?" the young (not really so young any more) man said. "I'm afraid I don't understand."

"Yes, cues," the bowling ball answered. "Visual cues, auditory cues, even olfactory cues. Sensory cues of all sorts. You agree the universe is infinite? I mean in extent."

"I suppose so; I've never really thought about it."

"Think about it now," the bowling ball urged. With a mental arm it grasped his bicep. "Suppose yourself immortal and possessed of a galaxy-goblin spaceship requiring no fuel."

"Goblin?"

"I beg your pardon. I meant 'gobbling.' Out you go from —what do you call this place?" The bowling ball "took" a "card" from its "pocket."

" 'Earth,' " the not-so-young man said.

"Right. Earth. Out and out forever. Past . . .?"

"Stars, nebulae, galaxies, I guess. Cosmic dust."

"Precisely. And when you have passed them, what will you find ahead of you?"

The not-so-young man thought for a moment, then said, "The same sort of thing, I suppose."

"Cosmic dust, galaxies, nebulae, stars?"

"Yes."

"You agree, then, that the universe is of infinite extent?"

The bowling ball, for emphasis, slapped one of the arms of its chair, which, though it was constructed entirely of massy gold and conformed to an alien pattern of beauty and utility, was irresistibly comic.

"I do," the not-so-young man said, smiling a little.

"Very well. Now obviously a universe of infinite extent contains an infinite number of real objects of one kind or another—you need only go forward until you find something, and since we have agreed that the universe is infinite, you can always go forward some more."

The not-so-young man nodded.

"Now you will have noticed that *some* of the real objects in *this* universe produce sensory cues which you are able to detect—that is to say, you are not deaf, blind, and so forth. What is one half of infinity?"

"Infinity," the not-really-so-young-anymore man answered promptly.

"And half of that? Or for that matter a millionth part of it."

"Still infinite." (He had once been forced to take a course in mathematics.)

"Then *if any part* of the sensory cues produced by that infinite number of real objects reaches you, you are confronted by an infinite array of sensory cues."

After a moment the not-so-young man nodded again, then added, "If you are right—and I have to admit I can't see where you could be wrong—I'm surprised I'm not overwhelmed."

"Because," the bowling ball told him, "you are incapable of reacting to or even noticing more than a very small fraction of the total. By an unconscious process you heed these and ignore everything else. Let me give you an example: you are driving toward a railroad crossing—the warning light is flashing, and beside it a little girl is skipping rope. What do you do?"

"I stop," the not-so-young man said, "and let the train go past."

"Exactly. And when you arrive safely at home, it is because of the various sensory cues presented, the one you chose to act upon was that of the railway signal, while you never even noticed the traveling mountebank with his wand and coins and cups."

"You said it was a little girl skipping rope," the not-so-young man protested.

"The girl skipping rope was a cue you noticed without acting upon. We are discussing the cues you did not even notice. You wish to become a successful cartoonist, do you not?"

"More than anything else in the world," the not-so-young (really) man said, leaning forward. "And I must say I was beginning to wonder when we'd get to that."

"We already have. You are adept at pen and pencil sketches—unfortunately, they are not funny."

"They are funny. Listen, I realize that wherever you're from—"

"Deneb," said the bowling ball.

"I thought you said—"

"It doesn't matter," the bowling ball said quickly.

"Well, your sense of humor will naturally be different from ours, but look at this." The not-so-young man began to fumble in his portfolio, and the bowling ball said quickly (even more quickly than it had said "It doesn't matter"), "We have no sense of humor at all." It said this with a perfectly straight face.

"Well, have a look at this anyway." The not-so-young man

CUES   147

thrust a sketch in front of two of the bowling ball's holes. As it happened, they were the wrong holes.

"Hilarious."

"I don't think so, but I do think it's amusing. Yet no one wants it. How can you help me?"

"By making you aware—and only aware—of those clues which will enable you to depict the object you perceive in the most amusing possible way. You are sketching me?"

"I am," the not-so-young man said. "I've just gotten this idea for a sports equipment series."

"If you think I'm funny," the bowling ball said, "you ought to see the tennis racket."

"How did you know I thought you looked like a bowling ball? I've been noticing it all the time we've been talking. It's obtrusive, somehow."

"Only to cartoonists. Artists are likely to visualize us as dark spheres filled with stars."

"What about the holes?"

"Have you ever heard of the Coalstack Nebula?"

"Say, there's an idea in that."

"There's an idea in everything," the bowling ball said.

"I mean a cartoon idea—maybe a series." The not-so-young man was silent for a moment, thinking of a great many things—things that included a certain still-young woman and the drafting job to which he would soon be forced to return. "Listen," he said, "I want you to do this."

"Do what?"

"What you said—make me see only the funny cues."

"I already have," the bowling ball said. "Or at least, the process has already begun. You said earlier that you wished it, and the cost is very low."

"How low?" the not-so-young man asked, suddenly wary.

"Twenty-five cents."

"You're joking."

"Or nothing. Or whatever you like."

"I get it. I read a story like this once. I'll get rich, and then if I want to change back, you'll soak me for a fortune. Well, you're going to lose on this one, because I'm not going to want to, not ever. I'm going to have a hell of a good time, and I'm going to be famous and rich."

"You certainly are," the bowling ball agreed. "We'll even throw in an extra: your children will inherit your talent. They, too, will be rich and famous, though not, during your lifetime, as rich and famous as you, since you will be established earlier."

"Say, that's great. You're already doing it, you said? Is there anything else I have to do to qualify?"

"Nothing at all," the bowling ball said. "You are already beginning to respond only to the sensory cues I outlined, both in objects and situations. The process will be complete in a few days, and from that time forward we guarantee that where others see duty or ugliness or pathos or even beauty, you will see only humor. Good-by."

The not-so-young man left, and a second bowling ball rolled into the room; but the first did not perceive it as a bowling ball, nor was he himself so perceived. Instead each, for a moment, saw a fair blue world, mottled by clouds and rich with life. As it happened, at just that instant the not-so-young man returned and asked (grinning): "Say, since you're so nice, I wonder if you Denebians could stake *me* to twenty-five cents instead of the other way around. I'd like to tell my girl what's happening, but it's a toll call and I haven't got any change." Another customer pushed past him as he spoke, and the first bowling ball, after an inventory of her mind that required only a very small fraction of a second, began—as the new customer would later phrase it herself—to "think sexy." In answer to the not-so-young man's question, the second bowling ball turned from side to side. "I bed your pardon," he said. "We give no quarter."

And, still grinning, the not-so-young man withdrew.

SLUGGING IT OUT
Jack C. Haldeman II

The President sat behind his massive desk in the Oval Room, full attention on the yo-yo he was dangling. Concentration lined his young face as he bounced it up and down.

"Sir . . ." the door opened and an aide stepped in.

"Darn it, I told you never to interrupt me." The yo-yo, diverted, knocked a half-empty Coke bottle off the desk. Brown foam swirled across the floor.

"Sorry, sir," replied the aide, "but it's kind of important. The aliens have delivered an ultimatum."

"The aliens?" muttered the President, mopping up the mess with his handkerchief. "Oh, yes, those funny-looking slugs that landed in the Mall day before yesterday. I thought they'd left."

"Our intelligence crew discovered that they visited Rome, London, Moscow, and Peking after they left Washington."

"Tracked them with one of our new super-sophisticated electronic devices, I bet." A grin spread over the President's face.

"Well, not exactly." The aide shuffled his feet and picked some imaginary lint from his orange plastic see-through pants. "We saw it this morning on a TV newscast."

"ABC beat CIA again?"

"Afraid so, sir."

"Well, what do the slimy creatures want?"

"Mr. President, sir, I don't know quite how to tell you this, but they more or less want to take over the planet, enslave all the people, and turn the oceans into giant seaweed factories."

"Seaweed?"

"It appears to be a mild intoxicant for them."

"Where did I leave my intercom?" muttered the President as he pushed comic books around his desk top. "I have to get in touch with the Joint Chiefs of Staff."

"Begging your pardon, sir, but they are in your outer office. Have been since yesterday, on your orders, and I don't mind saying that they could use a bath or two."

"Well, don't just stand there with your mouth open, boy. Send them in."

"Right away, sir." The aide turned sharply on his heel, slipped a little on the spilled Coke, and stumbled towards the door.

As the three men entered the room, hidden door chimes played a slightly out of key version of "Hail to the Chief." Two of the three Joint Chiefs were dressed in the flashy electronic uniform of their service—rapidly shifting areas of blue and green over a background of white. The third was less well-dressed in a solid-color uniform. All were covered with rows of medals and ribbons. There was a great deal of clanking and confusion as they jostled each other in an attempt to get through the door first.

The President rose to take full advantage of his five-foot-seven frame. "Well, gentlemen, what do you have to report on this alien business?"

"This is definitely an Army problem," said the Secretary of the Army as he elbowed his way in front. "They are, after all, sitting on solid ground—our hallowed UNITED STATES SOIL

—paid for and kept free by the blood and sweat of so many of our fine Army men. Why, this is a shocking affront to the American Way of Life. We can't allow those greasy creatures to—"

"Sir," the Secretary of the Navy stepped forward, effectively stopping his esteemed colleague's soliloquy with a well-placed and surreptitious elbow to the diaphragm. "This is something that obviously only men of the Navy can take care of. After all, wasn't their *ship* first sighted by the Navy? Their slimy skin shows that they must spend a lot of time in the water, and who knows more about the water than the Navy?"

"All right, Sam," interrupted the President, walking around his desk, his crepe-soled shoes making sucking sounds as they squished across the Coke-soaked floor. "If you Navy men are so efficient, why wasn't I informed of the aliens' arrival until several hours after they had landed practically outside my window? Even the sidewalk venders were selling picture post cards of them by then."

"Well, uh, I have to admit that the report was somewhat delayed."

"Enough. It seems to me that the only logical branch qualified to handle this is the Space Force. Dave, how do you assess the situation?"

"Well, sir," the man in the cheap, solid-colored uniform stepped forward, "while it *is* true that they came in a spaceship, and they *are* aliens, we had kind of decided that it wasn't our problem." He turned a little red and looked away.

"You decided it wasn't your problem!" The President clutched at his throat and staggered back against the desk. "Just what do you mean?"

"Well, the truth of the matter is, begging your pardon, sir, that we don't feel that we are equipped to handle it." He was

SLUGGING IT OUT   153

wringing his hands in acute embarrassment.

"H-handle it? The most modern branch of the most modern service of the most modern country in the world can't handle a little thing like an invasion from outer space? In short, simple words, PLEASE TELL ME WHY!"

"Begging your pardon, sir, but you will recall that last year was a very bad year budget-wise. Cuts across the board and all that? Well, our fleet has been reduced this year. As a matter of fact, we have only one operable spacecraft. And no fuel for that one."

"Get some fuel and get that ship aloft."

"But, sir, it's a holiday and even if we could get some money for fuel, the crew won't load it today. You know how strong their union is."

"Here's the money for your stupid fuel." The President drew out his checkbook. "And tell Davis, their union president, that he had better get those men on the job—with triple time, of course—or the press learns the number of his Swiss bank account."

"Right away, sir." He grabbed the check, turned, and slipped quickly out the door, which once again played "Hail to the Chief" as the photo cell was tripped.

The massive spaceship squatted on the mall, dwarfing even the red, white, and blue flashing Washington Monument. Its lumpy garbage can appearance had drawn thousands of the curious. The mall hadn't been so crowded since the anti-war rally in '83 at the height of the Hawaiian intervention.

"All right, you guys," a bull horn roared over the general din, "I want all you National Guardsmen under General Den's command to form ranks over there by the front of the Museum of Holographic Art. This is a heavy moment for each of you.

The mayor, acting on his usual independent initiative, has called us out to meet this pressing situation. What was apparently a National emergency is actually a local one. This ship is in Washington territory and is now our problem. So line up, men, and don't bash anyone in uniform."

The Maryland and Virginia state police were approaching the mall from opposite ends. Wearing protective riot suits, they eyed each other suspiciously.

Six hundred Boy Scouts were wandering around doing good deeds, while an equal number of Girl Scouts did a brisk business selling cookies.

Large groups of people wandered aimlessly around the tree-lined mall. Placards reading "Aliens Go Home," "Earth Is for Earthlings," "Local 405 Opposes Alien Intervention," "Keep the Race Pure," and "Slugs Are Un-American" waved from the crowd. These were countered by signs stating "Aliens Are Our Friends," "Take a Slug to Lunch Today," and "Students for Peace with the Aliens." Small scuffles between the opposing factions broke out here and there, but Washington in August is just too hot for such continued physical exertion. Activity soon confined itself to the exchanging of obscene gestures.

Helicopters droned overhead. There were a couple of Army ones, but most belonged to local radio stations alerting their audience to the traffic hazards the aliens were causing. Fire trucks surrounded the area, the men unsure of their duty, positive only that their chief had ordered them to report.

There was a loud CLICK from the vicinity of the spaceship, followed by a series of squishy thuds that sounded exactly like a slimy pseudopod rasping against a microphone.

"Now hear this," boomed a metallic voice across the mall, "you will clear this area within fifteen minutes. We do not wish to kill you, but will not hesitate to do so if necessary."

Thirteen minutes later, after much confusion, the mall was cleared of the curious. Several thousand military men stayed nervously at their posts.

At precisely fifteen minutes post-announcement, a red gas was released near the base of the rocket. As it spread over a small area of the mall, the soldiers fell on contact. The use of gas masks did not significantly delay the reaction.

"It was foolish not to leave." The hidden speaker burst once more into life. "The gas we have just released will be fatal to your life-forms after five minutes' exposure. If this area is cleared, the gas will be neutralized. Should you choose to remain, we will release more gas and take whatever measures are necessary to assure that we remain unmolested."

The aliens viewed the resulting flurry of activity with detached interest from inside the ship. There were three of them —gray, shiny-skinned, with an indistinct shape that constantly shifted as they floated in transparent tanks filled with a viscous blue substance.

"Are you in contact with their president yet?" vorkled one of the occupants to their computer.

"Not yet. Their communication system is quite archaic and inefficient. All I can receive are recorded messages," clicked the computer in return.

"Release the antedote gas. The area is cleared."

"Gas released."

Through the view screen a green gas could be seen to flow around the ground. The men stirred, but did not yet rise.

"It's a shame these humans are essential to our plans; they appear to be most undependable," vorkled the middle one as he extended a pseudopod aimlessly.

"True," answered another. "However, if we were forced to mechanize the operation, it would push us over the budget." He quickly sucked in an appendage at the thought.

"Computer, when you reach the President, arrange an immediate meeting. I want to talk with him and whoever else is necessary to confirm the surrender of this planet."

"Very good. I assume you wish them to board the ship."

"Correct. It is too hot to venture unnecessarily outside. Seal us off and adjust the atmosphere in here for them."

"This is getting us nowhere!" The President slammed his fist down as he suddenly stood up at the end of the long, crowded table. "Shut up, all of you. This bickering has got to stop. I have one hour before the meeting and I need *ideas*—not arguments."

"Mr. President, I think I have the answer." An old man with a flowing white beard stood up.

"And just who are you?"

"Professor Howell, the world's most experienced researcher in molluscoidal physiology. Slugs, to you." The old man sighed as he removed his glasses.

"And what do you propose?"

"Sprinkle salt on them."

"Nuts," said the President. "Advisers I need and crackpots they send me." He deciphered the intricate medallion the old man was wearing and correctly placed him with the Mobilization and Militarization of American Scientists faction.

"You MAMAS boys are all alike—all crazy as loons. When the aliens first arrived, we believed your wild story of catching slugs in a saucer of beer. So I had the reflecting pool drained and filled with five million gallons of imported beer. You know the results of that. *Six hundred* arrests for drunk and disorderly conduct in one night and we didn't catch a single slug. Besides, it killed all the goldfish."

"Well, it always worked for my mother."

"Aggg . . . What about the Space Force?"

"We have the ship up now, sir. It's hovering above Hot Springs, Arkansas, and can bring instant forces to bear."

"What armaments are aboard?"

"The standard laser banks should be sufficient. If we need more, there is the Ultimate Weapon."

"What is that?"

"I'm not sure, sir. I believe it has something to do with extra dimensions, or something like that. The only person with a high enough security clearance to know much about it is the fellow who built it. We figured anyone with that much information would be dangerous walking around, so we put him under lock and key six years ago."

"Get him here!"

"Well, sir, he starved to death three years ago. The neighbors forgot to feed him while we were on vacation."

"Oh, come on, doesn't anyone have *any* ideas?"

"There is one thing that might help us now." A distinguished-looking gentleman in the purple uniform of a physician leaned back in his chair. "When you were operated on last year for that stomach trouble"—the doctor stared at the blank note pad in front of him—"you remember it was just after the defeat of the impeachment proceedings. It, uh, well . . ."

"Get on with it."

"Well, the military thought that perhaps your frame of mind had been altered by that near miss at impeachment and they, uh, wanted some assurance that you wouldn't act against the best interest of the country. So I was forced into a little bit of extra surgery."

The President's hand involuntarily flew to his side.

"I really didn't want to," stammered the doctor. "But as they pointed out, I *do* have relatives living in Washington. So I performed this extra surgery—minor for one of my skill. I replaced a section of your small intestine with that new plastic nuclear explosive."

Gasps went around the table. The President jerked bolt upright—a real gut reaction. The room exploded with murmurs, and the white-faced President gingerly tapped his abdomen.

"I didn't want to do it, but *he* forced me." He pointed across the table to the Secretary of the Army, who rocked back as if struck.

"I couldn't help it!" the general shouted. "It had to be done. The people needed protection. It is to your credit that only once or twice have I considered detonating the device."

The President shook as he remembered all the times that he had beaten the general at checkers.

"But I see what the doctor is driving at." The general removed his watch. "*You* could detonate the explosive during the meeting if things get hopeless. There is enough force in your belly to level a ten-block area—that could finish off the slugs."

He handed the watch, a Spiro Agnew collectors' item, to the President. "Just set the hands to two o'clock and press the stem. That's all."

The President cradled the watch gently in his hands as he shakily adjourned the meeting.

"You must admit our superior forces make resistance futile," vorkled one of the aliens as he pointedly tied an eyestalk in knots.

SLUGGING IT OUT   159

Six humans stood in the room staring at the tank-enclosed creatures. It was impossible to tell which slug was talking. They all looked alike.

"We demand an immediate halt to hostilities against us. Males over the age of ten will be pressed into service setting up and operating the seaweed harvesting facilities. The machinery is fairly complex, but we are confident you will be able to handle it. After we thin out the female population to the minimal survival number, they will care for the infants and run the trivial aspects of the work camps. You will, of course, leave all the cities and live in minimal comfort camps that you will construct near the seas."

The computer clicked in. "Sensors pick up the approach of a laser-equipped ship."

"Throw up the screen."

"Their lasers have been deployed."

Pause.

"They have destroyed the Pentagon and half of Arlington Cemetery. They seem to lack accuracy."

Of the group in the ship, only the President was aware that the Space Force would now deploy the Ultimate Weapon, whatever that was.

"Incredible!" came the computer's excited voice. "They have just temporalized the Washington Monument into Spacial Dimension 1244. Look! There goes the Lincoln Memorial."

"Isn't SD1244 where we toss our garbage?" vorkled a slug.

"Yes," answered the computer. "Total failures. We are employing no defensive measures except the screen, and they haven't even come close. Look! Their ship just ran into its own beam. It has joined the rest of the garbage."

"Enough of your silly games. Now to details. We expect

to cut the male population in half—that should be enough for our needs. The female population, being mostly unnecessary for our plans, will be cut to a greater degree."

The President hardly listened. His moment of truth and glory had arrived. There was nothing to do but carry out the desperation plan. Slowly he moved Spiro Agnew's hands to two o'clock.

He pressed the stem.

The Prime Minister of England tapped his bowler.

The Russian Premier flicked a hidden switch on his tie clasp.

The Indian Minister touched the ruby in her forehead.

The African Supreme Co-ordinator clicked his heels together.

The Chinese Ambassador scratched his armpit.

And nothing happened.

A few snaps and fizzes, but with the exception of the sudden disintegration of the Prime Minister's bowler, nothing of note took place.

"My sensors somewhat belatedly detect that all the Earthlings carry on or within themselves destructive devices. They are all poorly constructed and inoperable."

"Stars!" exclaimed one slug as he turned a vivid sickly green. "They can't even manage a decent suicide attempt. These inferior beings have all the ingenuity and skill of a Guelphian crab-herder."

"Your continued resistance is futile. Such incompetence is no match for our superior technology and intelligence. We shall show your world what power we hold by executing you. I think we should do it on the steps of your Capitol Building. Yes, a public execution covered by your television networks should serve our purposes admirably."

The President restrained an impulse to wave at the TV cameras that followed their slow march to the Capitol steps. After all, this was serious business—life and death, as a matter of fact. Besides, the elections were over a year away. He did manage a dignified stance in spite of a stomach ache he hoped was psychological.

"Keep moving," vorkled one of the slugs. "Our life support systems are not extremely comfortable."

The aliens crept clumsily along the ground enclosed in the blue liquid held in place by their individual force fields. These fields, the humans had been told, were generated by an apparatus smaller than a pack of matches and besides holding the liquid in place were impervious to direct hydrogen bomb blasts, laser beams, and assorted projectiles.

As they reached the base of the steps, the President heard the sputter-pop of an out-of-tune helicopter. All heads and eyestalks turned towards Constitution Avenue as a thirty-five-year-old helicopter clumsily cleared the trees and rose over the mall.

"One of MAMAS boys," muttered the President, regretting for a moment having cut their funds last year.

"Our screens are secure," vorkled a slug. "Continue with the ceremony."

The helicopter had started a noisy flight down the mall. A large blue cylinder was strapped underneath it, and from a series of holes punched in the trailing end a white substance was flowing out. Caught by the breeze, it billowed in huge clouds, sweeping over everything in sight.

"Sodium!" vorkled a slug.

"Chloride!" vorkled another.

"Salt!" exclaimed the President as he licked the back of his hand.

The little white grains easily penetrated the laser-proof force fields. With a great thrashing of pseudopods, the slugs turned a foamy white and exploded—showering everyone around.

The blowing salt worked its way into the mostly fluid-filled interior of the alien's spacecraft. The ship rocked back and forth, its top foaming like an angry beer can. With a tremendous roar the ship blew apart. The mall was awash with flying fluid.

As the alien mist settled on the President, he grabbed an umbrella from a nearby Girl Scout. He grumbled as he raised it, for he had always been susceptible to summer colds.

"When it rains, it pours," he muttered.

FLAUNA
Raymond F. Jones

Flauna Bryson's family moved next door to my folks when Flauna and I were little. I can remember the very first time I saw her. The moving van had pulled up to the house, and the men had put out the long boards like a sort of gangplank to wheel things inside. When the van was about half emptied, Mrs. Bryson drove up with Flauna.

I watched the new neighbors from our front window. Mrs. Bryson got out of the car, as pretty as the ladies in my mother's dress catalogues. Flauna jumped out and ran to the moving van to claim a doll buggy that was just brought out. I can remember even now how her long, blonde hair bounced as she ran. She wore some kind of white dress that seemed fluffy as a cloud, and it had some pink things somewhere on it. That's the way I always remember her, bouncing, laughing, fluffy, and white. I can't remember her ever wearing anything really grubby, although of course she did when she scrubbed the apartment and nursed her little garden in the back yard during those terribly short years of our marriage.

Flauna was five when I first saw her, and I was just a little more. And I think I knew then that I would love her forever.

I could not admit it, of course. That sort of knowledge would have been too great a burden to bear in childhood. So, instead, I fought with her. And she fought back.

165

Our parents couldn't understand it. They wanted desperately to be good neighbors. Mrs. Bryson volunteered to join the car pool to take us and a couple of other kids to kindergarten. The very first day Flauna and I started quarreling and hitting each other in the car. Mrs. Bryson, who seemed too beautiful to be driving a carful of kids to school, stopped at least four times and scolded us both, but mostly Flauna. It didn't do any good; we just kept on hitting and shouting at each other all the way, like a couple of real brats.

My mother, who was nice but not nearly so pretty as Flauna's mother, drove us the next day, and it was the same, except that I was the one who got the most scolding. Flauna sat in the corner of the back seat and pulled faces at me and stuck her tongue out when my mother wasn't looking.

Our mothers gave up in despair and divided the car pool again. My mother continued as before. Flauna's mother took Flauna by herself.

It didn't matter. Flauna and I were at each other every chance we got in school. One time I plastered a gob of library paste in that long, golden hair of hers. She didn't cry. She just scribbled all over my schoolwork with a thick, black felt pen.

I threw mud on her one time when she had a brand-new Easter dress, white with pink blossoms and bows.

She sprayed a can of gold paint on a new suit of mine when my mother had some things hanging on the line outside while she cleaned my closet.

We all but killed each other, my beautiful Flauna and I.

Her imagination was wild. She said things at times that were beyond even childish fancy. One summer night when we were playing in her back yard later than we were usually allowed out, she looked up to the sky and pointed to a star. "I was on a world belonging to that star last night," she said. "I went there, and I saw a beautiful city, all white and gold, and people were so happy there."

"You're crazy," I said. "You couldn't go to a star. You haven't got any rocket ship. And, besides, they can't go that far. You had a dream."

"It wasn't a dream," she said furiously. "I went to a star. I saw cities and people. If you don't believe me, you can just go on home, Paul Norbert!"

I went home. She never mentioned her star dreams again. Not then.

Our parents became very good friends. They had dinners and parties and back yard get-togethers. Through it all, Flauna and I played and fought and screamed at each other almost to the point of destruction. We had to deny the need we had in each other, which we could not dare to look upon or admit to ourselves. In those years we tried to destroy what we could not endure.

That phase lasted until we were about twelve. Then we sort of ignored each other for the next couple of years, pretending the other didn't exist, although we still saw each other at school and over the fence at home.

Then, one day when we were almost fifteen, I asked her to go to a school dance. She acted almost shy and happy, as if I were some new boy who was the campus catch instead of the one she had fought with since we were in kindergarten.

I felt a catch in my throat when I called for her that night. She looked so pretty I couldn't believe it. My father drove us and came to pick us up. I seemed almost on the verge of admitting to myself that Flauna was the other half of my life. She seemed to feel the same. Then something happened, and we were at it again. Somewhere during the middle of the evening, something went wrong and it was all just as before. Only we didn't scream and hit each other now. We just grew cold and bitter, and we waited silently for my father to come and get us.

When he saw us, he sighed as if he recognized the old familiar situation, but he said nothing. He just drove us home, and I walked Flauna stiffly to her door, saw her inside, and turned and walked to my own place.

Flauna's mother told my mother that Flauna cried all night. She alternately swore she'd kill me, and that she would never look at me again as long as she lived.

Neither of us ever recalled exactly what went wrong on that first date of ours.

After that disaster I dated other girls, and Flauna went with other boys, and for another year or so we pretended the other didn't exist.

Flauna seemed to have a kind of light that surrounded her as she moved through her high school years. People were happy when they were around her. And they were around her all the time. She was the most popular girl in the whole school, but nobody was jealous of her. She had to brush off the boys who pestered her for dates. Some were the shy types who politely requested her to go to a show or a dance. Others were the big-men-on-campus types who told her they were picking her up for a big time next Saturday night. She handled them all the same, and picked carefully the companions that suited her taste.

Then she and I tried again. She got a fancy new bicycle for her seventeenth birthday. I still had my old clunker that I'd torn down and put together and repainted a million times since I was twelve. We just started riding around the streets in our neighborhood together, and that seemed to be something we could endure.

We took longer rides, into the hills above our town, and Dad began letting me have the car, and Flauna and I took some long afternoon picnics and hikes together. That summer she was seventeen was really the beginning for us; twelve long years after I first saw the little blonde girl chasing the moving man to get her doll buggy out of the van.

Our *real* closeness started then, yes, but it wasn't smooth. I got jealous, because I began to think of her as my girl, and she continued seeing others. I planned to go to the Spring dance with her. I had some new clothes and had saved up enough money for a real evening. But I had just sort of taken it for granted she'd be going with me. I didn't ask her until the week before, and she said she already had a date.

I was furious. I found out who it was. Tom Masters. I asked him what he thought he was doing asking my girl to the dance with him. I ordered him to break it off.

Tom wasn't as big as I was, but he could fight better. We both ended up with a good beating, a session with the principal, five days' suspension from school. And neither of us went to the dance.

Flauna went with someone else.

There was a period of coolness after that. Then we came back together. And now we started to get frightened again. Some of our friends were getting married. It was time to be thinking about that. We dated, we went to shows, to dances, for long rides. We talked endlessly—about everything but the way we felt. We even laughed about the fights we'd had as children, and we told each other that crazy sort of thing was certainly behind us forever.

But I didn't tell her how much I loved her.

Somebody else told her he did. She started going with a big football type, the kind the colleges buy with free scholarships and promises from the alumni to set up a sand and gravel business after graduation. This guy, Brad Hinkle, started coming around more and more until I couldn't even get a date with Flauna two weeks ahead.

Finally, he even boasted he was marrying Flauna Bryson.

I tried the same treatment I'd given Tom Masters. I shouldn't have done that, but I didn't know what else to do. It cost me three days in the hospital and seven stitches under my left eye.

But at least Flauna came to see me.

"What's the matter with you, you ape," she cried. "You haven't got any more sense in your head than when we used to throw rocks at each other over the back fence!"

"Flauna—you aren't going to marry that jackass—"

"He hasn't asked me."

"He's telling everybody you are."

She looked pensive. "I might, then."

"Flauna—look—you can't do that. It's been me and you ever since we yapped at each other through the back fence when we were kids. It's me, Paul Norbert, the guy that used to put paste in your hair and get his clothes sprayed with gold paint. You couldn't marry anybody else. It—it would be against Nature."

"Do you want me to marry you, Paul?"

"I'm saying it, aren't I?"

"No, you're not."

I reached out and pulled her down, and I didn't care if she did bump my eye and open the cut again. For the first time in my life I allowed myself to recognize my immense need of her. I knew then what had happened inside me that first day I saw her when we were five years old.

I knew then why I had had to fight with her all those years, and torment her and pretend I couldn't stand her. I had to wait until I grew up enough to understand such a vast need as I had of her.

And I knew it was the same for her. She had fought back for the same reason. "Will you marry me, Flauna?" I asked.

"Yes, I will, Paul. Why didn't you ever say it before? Why didn't you ever ask me?"

"It wasn't time, darling," I said. "It wasn't time until now."

She nodded against my bruised jaw, and I knew she understood what I was saying.

Even then, we waited a couple more years, until I got halfway through my college work. She became a dental assistant and saved up so we could get a start. And then we were finally married, when I was twenty, and she was not quite that age herself.

The sudden unleashing of our great need for one another was almost frightening. Where we had only sensed it before, we now looked upon the full depth of it and knew how empty the world had always been until now. Our loving, at times, was almost like an enormous struggle to consume one another, while at the same time we knew we had to hold each other forever.

For a year we loved, as we were sure no other lovers had ever loved. We had an apartment near the campus, prisonlike in its dullness and uniformity with a thousand other little one-bedroom cells of the same kind. But it was no prison to us. It was a magic world which we knew had never been entered before by mortal beings.

Flauna wanted to grow things, and she dug up the little five by ten foot space that was our own private back yard and made a garden out of it. She could really grow things, too. It seemed as if she had only to stand on the ground and green things would come up all around her. We had so many flowers in the apartment and so many fresh vegetables on the table all that summer that I was sure she must be cultivating at least a half acre.

When fall came, the little garden withered, and we picked the last tomatoes together just before the frost hit them. Then we watched from the apartment windows as dry leaves swirled across the parking lot and snow finally covered the ground. It was pure magic, watching the changing world from our private domain. We knew our love would go on forever.

One morning, in the Winter, after we had gone to sleep in the attitude of love, I awoke to feel her lying in my arms strangely different. Her long, sweet legs, sprawled across me, felt cold and limp. Her naked back was chill, and her head on my chest was a lifeless weight. In panic I rolled her over and felt beneath her breast for the beat of her heart.

There was none.

We'd had no occasion to establish a relationship with a family doctor. I supposed there was one somewhere on the campus, but I didn't know how to reach him.

I grabbed the phone and called Flauna's mother.

"Mrs. Bryson—this is Paul. Something's wrong with Flauna. I don't know what it is. Do you have a doctor who knows her?"

Flauna's mother didn't panic. She caught her breath, and there seemed the hint of some strange fear in her voice. "What has happened, Paul? Tell me what her symptoms are."

"She's unconscious. And cold. I can't even feel a pulse."

"Don't call a doctor. She'll be all right. I'll come right over. It'll take me only fifteen minutes."

"She may be dying—or already dead!"

"Please believe me, Paul. It's something—something that's happened before. She's going to be all right. I know how to handle it."

She hung up the phone. I didn't know whether to believe her or not. Flauna could be dying—and every minute might make a difference.

I replaced the phone and turned back to my love. She did not look dead, or even ill. She seemed only sleeping, except for the whiteness of her flesh and the coldness. She even seemed to be smiling, as if she were having a pleasant dream.

I thought of putting a gown on her, but I was afraid I might hurt her. I covered her warmly with a blanket. By the time I had finished dressing, Mrs. Bryson was ringing the bell.

Her face was white and tense. She looked strangely like Flauna herself. "Let me see her," she said. "The faster we are able to act, the easier it may be."

I didn't know what she was talking about. I followed as she made her way purposefully to the bedroom.

She laid her coat on a chair and sat on the bed beside Flauna. She reached under the cover and drew out Flauna's cold hand and held it in her own.

"Flauna," she said softly. "This is Mother. I've come to take you back. Come back with me, Flauna. You've left Paul alone. He needs you—and you need him."

A flicker of understanding seemed to cross Flauna's face. Her smile broadened just a little, as if she wanted to say something. Then it died away, and a frown took its place.

Mrs. Bryson saw it, too. She spoke more intensely. "Flauna! Hear me, Flauna! This is your mother. I've come to take you back. You must come back with me to Paul, who loves you. You can't leave him alone this way."

Flauna's face bore an expression of despair, as if she were being torn to choose between two things, both of which she wanted desperately.

Mrs. Bryson seemed exhausted and worried. "Perhaps you'd better go out to the other room," she said to me. "This may take a little longer than I thought."

"No. I want to stay. What is wrong with Flauna? Is she in some kind of trance? Is she ill?"

"She's not in a trance," said Mrs. Bryson wearily. "And she's not ill. I'll try to explain it to you someday, Paul. But right now I must bring her back as quickly as possible. She's a strong-willed girl—as I guess you know well enough."

"Doesn't she—want—to recover?" I didn't know how to say it. I didn't know how to ask whether Flauna had any volition concerning the state she was in.

"She doesn't know what she wants. Now, I mustn't talk any more."

Mrs. Bryson closed her eyes and held Flauna's hand against her cheek. I was frightened and worried. Although her mother seemed to think it was something she could simply be talked out of, I still wasn't even sure Flauna was more than barely alive. I moved closer, straining to catch a change of expression in Flauna's face, trying to hear the whispered words of her mother.

"This is not for you, Flauna," Mrs. Bryson said. "It will only waste your being, and leave you empty. You've got Paul, and he can give you life and happiness. But it's cruel to leave him this way. You can't live two lives, Flauna. Come back to the one that can give you happiness."

I saw tears edging slowly down the cheeks of Mrs. Bryson. She had always been so young and beautiful, even as Flauna herself. But now I saw the lines of age that I had never seen before. It was as if she had grown ten years older since I saw her last.

After another silence she opened her eyes, blinking as if having trouble recognizing me after a long absence. "She will be all right," she said at last in a very tired voice. "Flauna will be all right."

She put her daughter's arm under the cover again and patted her gently with infinite love. She drew back and waited. I had the feeling that she had been expecting—and dreading—this event to happen.

Whatever it was.

Flauna's face showed a trace now of changing expression. The color was returning to her flesh. There was movement under the cover as she shifted to a new position. I rushed forward to touch her, but Mrs. Bryson stopped me.

"You must be very careful. An abrupt awakening can be very traumatic. Just let her return at her own pace now."

"But what was the matter with her? Tell me that. Please!"

"She has—illusions. Dreams, shall we say, of an incredibly fantastic nature. They are deeper than any ordinary dreams of sleep. They carry a far more potent experience than ordinary dreams. You will see in a moment."

I waited. Flauna slowly opened her eyes. She looked about the room as if having difficulty recognizing where she was. Then she saw me and smiled in her soft, loving way that told me nothing had changed between us.

"Paul." She extended an arm from under the covers and took my hand in hers. "Oh, Paul, I wish you could have gone with me." She turned to Mrs. Bryson. "Mother, it was the most beautiful experience I've ever had—and you had to make me come back!"

"You wanted to come back, didn't you—to Paul?"

"Oh, yes—but can't he go with me next time? Isn't there some way he can go with me and see the worlds I have seen?"

"No, darling." Mrs. Bryson shook her head. "There must never be a next time. Paul cannot go, and you must never go again. You'll risk everything you have if you let yourself do that any more."

"Oh, why, Mother—? It is so beautiful. So free. The whole Universe is mine!

"It is a world of springtime. There's never been anything so beautiful. There are friends there. They welcomed me. There was happiness and joy—such as Heaven must contain."

"It's not real, Flauna. Paul cannot go there. I and your father cannot go there."

"*You* can go. You know that. Why can't they? Why can't everyone? I don't understand it. I don't want to leave Paul. I don't want to leave you and Dad. But why can't everyone go?"

"Where is this world?" I said. "Tell me where I would have to go to find this world of springtime you have seen."

She smiled at me as if I were a child. "You couldn't find it as you are now. Your science wouldn't let you. It's out beyond the stars. Beyond Alpha Centauri. Beyond Andromeda."

"But they're—"

"Yes," she laughed. "You see, your science says they are too far, too many light-years away to be grasped in an instant. But that's not true, Paul. There are ways—Oh, I wish you could see!" Her voice broke in a sob.

Vividly now I remembered her fantasies that night when we were children. "I went to that star last night," she had said. But they were the dream fantasies of a child.

Mrs. Bryson came near and touched her arm. Her voice was severe. "Never again, Flauna. Do you understand me? Never again, or you will lose everything. Promise me!"

Flauna wiped her tears on the sheet. She looked up at me gravely. "You really can't go, can you, Paul?"

"No. I can't go, darling. Only you."

"Then I won't go, either. I'm sorry I left you. I will never go again."

She turned over and closed her eyes as if to sleep. Her mother nodded to me, and we went out to the living room, closing the door softly behind us.

I turned to Mrs. Bryson. "What in the world kind of experience is that?" I asked. "Surely it's something that needs medical attention. We should get her to a psychiatrist. These fantasies—"

Mrs. Bryson shook her head. "There's no need. Flauna can control it—if she wants to. And if she doesn't want to, there's nothing a psychiatrist can do for her."

"But living in a world of fantasy like this is a mental sickness of the worst kind. Why didn't you ever tell me?"

"I thought it would never happen, Paul. Don't blame me. A mother does what she thinks best for her child. Flauna was so in love with you I didn't want to risk the chance of her losing you."

"I'm not blaming you. I just want Flauna's happiness and well being."

"She'll be all right. I promise you she will. It's not a sickness. But it's not anything the doctors can understand, either. Paul—why don't you and Flauna have a child? I think a baby would do her more good than anything."

"We've talked about it. But we don't see how we can afford it at this time."

"We'll help you. Don't tell her, but let us know what you need."

"We couldn't do that."

"It's for Flauna. Let us help."

"All right. We'll talk about it. I'll let you know."

Flauna got up and dressed while her mother and I talked. When Mrs. Bryson had gone, Flauna made breakfast and acted as if nothing unusual had happened. The only sign was that she seemed even more gay and happy than usual, if that were possible.

She hurried breakfast, and she hurried me. "You'll be late for your first class if you don't move faster, Sleepyhead," she said.

I took her in my arms and held her close. "Don't leave me like that again," I said.

"I won't, darling."

"Promise?"

"Promise."

"There's something we talked about a long time ago. I think we ought to talk about it some more."

"What's that?"

"A baby."

"Oh, Paul, we decided to wait until you were finished with school."

"I don't think we ought to wait so long. We can manage. Look at all the kids in this building. Their parents seem to be doing all right."

"You've got to get to class. We can't stand here deciding to have a baby now."

I laughed at her earnest, pixie frown of despair about getting me out of the apartment. I kissed her gently. "Think about it today, and we'll talk about it some more tonight."

"You'll have to finish school first," she called after me. "We'll have to wait until then."

We talked about it some more that night, and there really wasn't much to talk about. I wanted a little girl Flauna, and she wanted a little boy Paul. And while we talked we loved, and it went on the whole night long. When morning came, we knew we had made the most wonderful baby in the world.

I won. It was a little blonde girl who looked so much like Flauna that I couldn't help remembering the little Flauna I had first seen so long ago.

She wouldn't hear of the baby being named for her, although I would have liked it. Her mother didn't want the name used again, either, for some reason she seemed to feel unreasonably strong about.

I didn't press it. We named the baby Laura, and we loved her. And regardless of her name, she looked more like Flauna every day.

The nightmare experience when I had awakened with Flauna cold and unconscious was almost forgotten. Nothing like it had happened all during her pregnancy or after. And now she had Laura, and we were happy in our love. Flauna's mother and I had never spoken of it again. I was so sure it would never happen again.

But it did.

I came home early one afternoon because a class had been canceled as a result of a professor's illness. The door of the apartment was locked. I could hear Laura crying faintly inside. Flauna didn't answer, and I let myself in with my key.

I found the baby in her crib, wet and unhappy. And on the bed Flauna lay sprawled and unconscious. The same as before.

I felt a chill crawl over my back.

"Flauna!" I yelled at her in mixed panic and anger.

Anger because I remembered her mother's statement that Flauna could control it if she wanted to.

Panic because something had touched her and held her in its power. Something I could not name or understand or combat.

I sat on the edge of the bed and shook her shoulders roughly. "Flauna!" I cried. "Flauna—come out of it. You've got to take care of the baby. Where are you, Flauna? Come back to us, my darling—come back to us—"

I put my hands under her shoulders and pressed my face against her breast, crying in fear and despair. I knew Mrs. Bryson had been right; this was no condition the medical profession could understand or cope with. It had something to do with evils, and spells, and wanderings of the mind.

I could hear a faint heartbeat beneath my ear. She was still alive. I reached for the phone and called her mother. "Flauna's gone again," I said.

"I thought it was over," Mrs. Bryson said in despair. "I thought it would not happen again."

"What shall I do? Is there anything I can do until you get here?"

"Is the baby all right?"

"Yes—I guess so. She's crying and wet. I haven't had time to change her."

"Take care of Laura, Paul. I'll—I'll talk to Flauna—"

"You'll come right over?"

"I won't need to. I can talk to her without coming. It will be all right again. I promise you, Paul."

I hung up, not knowing what to believe. She had promised before, but her promise had failed. And how could she talk with

Flauna from her home two miles away? As easily, perhaps, as she had talked to Flauna and brought her out of the coma the first day I had seen it.

I changed the baby quickly and warmed a bottle and settled her in the crib again. She remained quiet. I returned to Flauna's side. She had not moved, but her eyelids were beginning to twitch. Then suddenly her whole body twisted in an agony of anger and she burst out venomously, "Mother—go away, and let me alone! I'm happy here. I'll come back when I'm ready. Let me alone! You make me hate you when you force me back."

There was a moment of quiet as she lay relaxed once more. I had the feeling she was listening. Then she smiled wanly, her eyes still closed. "Paul—" she said. "And our Laura—they do need me. I'm so selfish to leave them, I know. What can I do, Mother? Tell me what to do."

Her anguish seemed beyond anything I could imagine. Whatever fantasy had her in its grip was so real that the thought of giving it up seemed agony to her.

She fell quiet again, and her breathing became normal and regular, as if she were asleep. The anguish disappeared from her face, and she seemed at peace once more. Abruptly, her eyes opened, as if she had just awakened from a sleep.

"Paul—" She smiled and held out her arms. "What are you doing home so early? I didn't expect you."

The happiness on her face was as if the memory of paradise clung to her mind. And now the pain was mine because some alien dream could bring such happiness to her.

"I had a business class canceled out this afternoon," I said. She sat up. "Laura—is the baby all right?"

"I changed her and gave her a bottle. She's all right."

"Oh, thanks, darling. I guess I must have gone to sleep. I

meant to lie down only a minute."

"Flauna—" I stood by the bed and looked sternly at her. "Flauna, you've been away again—"

Her face saddened. "I'm sorry, Paul. I didn't want you to know."

"But you promised! You promised you wouldn't do it again." And then a sickness struck me. "How long have you been doing this, Flauna?"

"Only a few times. I started again right after the baby was born. Oh, Paul—if you understood what it was like, you wouldn't ask me to stop. So few people can do it—so few ever know what an experience it is."

"Plenty of people get lost in the corridors of their minds and can't find their way out. A mind that lives in fantasy is no special thing, darling. Millions of people are tormented by it. It's a sickness. If you can't stop, we've got to find help for you."

She laid her hand on my arm. "Paul—Paul—do you think I'm just having illusions? Do you think these worlds of happiness are only fantasies?"

"What else can they be?" I waved my hands toward the walls of the room. "This is real. Here's the only reality that exists. Me—our baby—our apartment—our love. Is there anything real besides these things you can see and feel?"

She nodded dreamily. "Yes, there are other things just as real. This gift of mine, this gift of star roaming is real."

"This what? What did you call it? Star roaming?"

"Yes. At first I thought it must be something everyone had. Do you know when I first knew they didn't?"

"When?"

"At the time we were in the back yard when we were children and you called me crazy because I told you I had been to a star. That was when I began to learn I was different. I'm sorry you can't go with me, Paul."

"Where do you go?" I asked gently. "Just where do you go?"

"I told you the first time. To the stars—and beyond. There's nowhere in space that a Star Roamer cannot go. There's no splendor in all the Universe that I cannot see, all in a moment's time. The speed of light is snail's pace to a Star Roamer."

"And you can visit the worlds? The Moon, Mars—"

"They're the dead ones. I like to go where there are people —happy, glorious people who know how to make so much more of their lives than we do here. Oh, if you could only go with me, we would never come back!"

Her intensity frightened me. "I can't go. You and I have loved each other all our lives. Isn't that enough to keep you here?"

"Don't ask me that way. I'm not taking anything from you by going out there once in a while, visiting worlds where others know me and love me, too. I'll always come back. Do you know something?"

"What?"

"Our baby will be a Star Roamer, too! The females always are. I'll teach her how to find her way among the stars. Oh, it will be such fun visiting the worlds with her!"

"Flauna," I said, "are you going to take her from me, too?"

"Oh, Paul! You act as if I have deserted you. Why do you have to be that way? It's nothing."

"I'm frightened. I don't pretend to understand what you're telling me. But if you can control it, then give it up—for me and for Laura."

She shook her head slowly. "I love you with all my heart, but I can't give it up, nor will I deny it to our baby."

I skipped classes the next morning and went to see Mrs. Bryson. She wasn't surprised to see me. Her beautiful face was lined as if with some deep grief inside her.

"How is Flauna?" she said.

I sat down in the living room as she closed the door behind me. Through the window at the side I could see the yard my parents used to own, and the fence through which Flauna and I had fought so many childhood afternoons.

"What is a Star Roamer?" I said.

Mrs. Bryson spread her hands helplessly. "It's what Flauna is."

"And you?"

"Yes. I, too."

"I can't believe anything I've heard from you and Flauna. It's all insane. But tell me anyway what it means to you and Flauna."

"It's not insane. It's all too real. A Star Roamer—" She paused as if she could not continue. Then she seized some firm resolve and went on. "A Star Roamer doesn't belong to this world, Paul. A Star Roamer—there is another world from which we came."

"Flauna—?"

She shook her head. "Earth was one of the worlds I loved most when I first began to reach beyond my home. You see, when we visit, we take the form of the dominant life form on the planet. I took the form of an Earthwoman, of course. And I amused myself by replicating the most beautiful and desirable Earth creatures I could find. I think I did it very well.

"And then I did something utterly forbidden to us. I fell

in love with Flauna's father, an Earthman. I renounced my own world and vowed to give up roaming for him. I have kept that vow. He doesn't know me for what I am. He must never find out.

"I would have lived without children. But he would not. I was afraid for the combination of characteristics we might produce. But it turned out all right—almost. I have loved Flauna so. I wanted the gift to die in her because I knew it could only mean heartbreak to a hybrid such as she. I gave her my name, and then regretted it. Her name is Ef Launa and means Star Roamer in our language. That is why I opposed your giving it to Laura."

I remembered our childhood, that night in the dark with Flauna. "When did Flauna begin?"

"Why—you saw the first time, just after you were married. I was so hopeful it would never happen, because she had grown up without it."

I shook my head. "You didn't know, then. When she was six she looked at the sky and showed me a particular star. She said she had walked on a world belonging to that star the night before. I told her she was crazy."

Mrs. Bryson paled. "I didn't know. I didn't dream—if that's true, she must have been doing it all her life. I've been living in a dream world of my own, thinking she had not learned the gift."

"How can I hold her? That's what I need you to tell me. Is there any way? I'm afraid. It's as if she's slipping away into some world where I can't reach her. It's like a glass wall growing thicker between us very hour. But I can't believe what you say is true. My reason tells me there must be some other explanation."

"If it is illusion for Flauna, I am deluded, too."

"Yes! Can't you believe the possibility that it is something controllable by psychiatric means?"

"I wish that were true. I would be a happier woman, and my heart would not ache for my daughter. Or for you. You see, Paul, I haven't been fair with you. I have used you to try to bring happiness to my daughter. When you were a little boy, I recognized in you someone Flauna could grow up to love. Someone who might be able to hold her. And I have cost you your happiness because you learned to love my daughter."

"You sound as if I have lost her already," I said.

"No. She loves you. Believe that, if you believe nothing else I have told you. And because she is of Earth, and because you love each other, it should be possible to hold her."

"But I can't fight it. She has already told me she will not give up star roaming."

"Let her go. The time will come when she will tire of it and stay with you. Never stop loving her and she will always be yours."

Out in the bright sunlight of day it was impossible to believe what I had just heard. Both Flauna and her mother were suffering some terrible delusion. Psychiatric help had to be the answer. But I knew of no way to persuade Flauna to get such help. Perhaps the university medical department could suggest something. I'd have to look into that.

For the present I decided to go along with Mrs. Bryson's suggestion. I would agree to Flauna's fantasy, pretend to believe in it, and listen to her experiences. Maybe that would help me find a clue to her recovery.

When I reached home that afternoon, Flauna, as always, acted as if there were nothing unusual in our lives. We had dinner and played with the baby and watched TV and went to bed early. While I held her snuggled close in my arms, I said, "I'm not going to oppose your star roaming, darling. I want you to feel free to do as you wish. Tell me about it when you care to. I'd like to share as much with you as I can."

She began to cry softly. "You'll never know how much I've longed to hear you say such a thing. I've wanted to talk to you about it, and I've never dared."

I learned then that it had been almost a daily thing for a long time. Sometimes she would slip away only for a few minutes in the middle of the night while I slept. Other times she would spend an hour or two in the afternoon while the baby was sleeping.

I controlled my feelings as best I could and watched her slip away into this state that was like some drugged trance. I had to pretend an interest and an excitement in the things she told me afterward. I listened to her imagined tales of wonder about fabulous cities on worlds light-years beyond the farthest galaxies. She told me of the people there, of their loves and their sorrows, their ambitions and disappointments. Their lives didn't sound too much different from the lives of Earthmen, only she picked worlds where aspirations were higher, and meanness was less, and human behavior was closer to its potential.

I always thought in terms of human beings, homo sapiens, until she offered one night to draw a sketch of the beings she consorted with in her fantasies.

"I found my home world," she said. "Mother would never tell me where she came from, but I found out for myself. Do you want to see what we look like?"

I nodded. She got a pad of graph paper I used in a class and began sketches with a soft pencil. As she drew, I felt a wave of horror. She was depicting an obscene travesty of a human being. There were appendages attached to a bulbous torso. Appendages that might have been used for walking or grasping according to need. A misshapen head lying neckless on that torso.

She drew two of them. "This one is me," she said. "This other one is—a friend of mine."

I had to laugh, to end the horror. "You and your friend look like some ripe fruit left out in the sun—about ready to pop open."

I was instantly sorry. She grabbed the sketch from my hands, angrier than I had ever seen her—since we threw rocks across the fence at each other.

"You laugh at everything I try to tell you! You make me think you want to hear and understand, and all the time you're ridiculing me and thinking I'm crazy. Well, *he* doesn't think I'm crazy!"

I tried to touch her, but she flinched away. "I'm sorry, darling," I said. "I wasn't making fun of you. The forms are just so unusual I couldn't imagine you looking like that. Forgive me, Flauna."

She accepted my apology, but I think it was from that moment forward that she changed.

More and more, for longer and longer periods, she was gone from me. I grew used to seeing her lying still and cold, as if all life had gone from her, while her mind wandered in realms of unreality. I no longer tried to rouse her and call her back. Sometimes I just sat silently watching her, waiting. And always, she opened her eyes with that smile of peace upon her lips as if she had experienced a taste of Heaven.

The more she succumbed to it, the more the thing deepened its hold on her, and I knew I had made a mistake in tolerating it. I should have gotten psychiatric help for her when it first renewed itself after Laura's birth. Now, the possibility of getting help for her seemed more remote than ever.

I persuaded her to talk about the images she had drawn for me that day, and she stuck the sketch to the dresser mirror. She told me, as her mother had, that her name was Ef Launa, the Star Roamer. She told me her friend was named Tavian, and she spoke of the obscene creature as "he," a male.

And slowly I knew that he was taking her from me.

Day by day I swung wildly between the conviction that Flauna and her mother both suffered extremely from hallucinations, delusions, or whatever name their fantasies might be called—between that and the terrifying doubt that maybe these were not illusions, after all.

Flauna's mother claimed she had come from this far world and loved an Earthman. Was it impossible that Flauna, her daughter of Earth, should return to the home of her kind and find love with one of her own? Was it impossible that she merely masqueraded in the form I knew and loved so dearly, and that her true form was the repulsive thing she had drawn for me? Did those creatures in the sketch love each other?

One day when I came home from classes and she roused from the coma in which I found her, I accused her of a new love.

She sat on the edge of the bed and avoided my eyes. "I've known I would have to tell you, Paul," she said. "But I didn't know how to do it. I'm going away. I'm not coming back. I'm going home."

I felt sick and wild inside. "You can't, Flauna. Does our life and our love mean nothing to you now? Do I mean nothing? And what of Laura?"

"Laura will join me when she is old enough."

"Flauna!"

She looked at me now. "I wouldn't have hurt you for anything in the world, Paul. Our life together has been the most wonderful thing I could have known on Earth. But it has to end. It's not my fault. Mother should never have mated with one not of her own kind. That's what she was taught, and it was true. She broke the laws, and you and I have suffered, as well as she and my father. She gave up star roaming because of her trespass. You'll never know what a sacrifice that is."

"You couldn't give it up for me?" I said. "Our love is not enough for that?"

"You don't understand. I have to have my own world. I have to have my own kind." There were tears on her face now.

"*This* is your world!" I cried angrily. "You're a human being. You're my wife, who loves me! And I love you."

She pointed to the picture on the mirror. "That's who I am. Do you love that?"

"No! I love you. That's not you—"

She rose and came to me. "I want to come into your arms —one last time, Paul. Take me in your arms."

It was insane, but I felt it was a last chance to hold her. We lay together and fought a love battle as furious as any we'd ever known. As she cried out in sweet pleasure, I thought of all the days gone by.

The mud I threw on her dress, and the paste I smeared in her hair.

The paint she sprayed on my suit.

I caressed her and kissed her and loved her and fought for her. I told the alien obscenity he could not have her, but it was as if she were dragged from my arms by a force like a dark shadow settling between us.

Slowly, while she clung to me and wept, she went limp in my arms, and cold.

Her mother knew it was different this time. She looked at me across the bed, her eyes bleak.
She won't be back, Paul.
You've lost.
I've lost.
Laura—
We've all lost.

The doctor certified cardiac arrest, and we buried her on a rainy Summer day.

It was a long time ago. So very long ago. Today Laura was seven, and we went to a birthday dinner and a movie, just she and I. She wore a white dress with pink things on it, like those her mother used to wear. Like the one I spattered with mud so many years ago. Her hair is long and golden, just as Flauna's was.

And walking home under the starlit sky she said, "Daddy, what's that bright star up there? Do you know I'm going to the stars someday? I'll bet Mama is up there among the stars. There are so many—do you think I could ever find which one is hers?"

The terrible chill that swept through me was not from the late Spring wind that blew in the tops of the trees around us.

TO SLEEP, PERCHANCE TO DREAM
Nancy Mackenroth

"Dreamer, awaken."

YaLin opened his eyes to the fiery red dawn and closed them again quickly as the images of the night came flooding back. He found that decision had been made while he slept. He knew what he must do.

"Awaken, my brother. The vigil is ended."

A smile tugged at YaLin's mouth. The old ways and their rituals did not rest well with his brother. YuAng was too casual and easy-going to recognize that the half-tender "my brother" had no place in the Ritual of Awakening.

When YaLin opened his eyes to the dawn once more and slowly rose to his feet, YuAng still had his back turned, facing the rising sun.

"The vigil is ended," YaLin said quietly. "I have slept long and awaken refreshed."

YuAng turned quickly to face the Dreamer. "The Dreams were good?" His shining voice changed ritual solemnity to joyful eagerness.

YaLin knew what he must do.

"There were no Dreams," he said harshly, and immediately started for the village. Bewildered, YuAng came slowly behind him. Many mornings they had come in off the desert together, brothers delighting in the dawn. But today they came

193

in apart as in the old days, Dreamer and Awakener.

The Old Dreamer stood outside his door, watching his sons return. He did not like their bearing.

"The Dreams were good?" he asked anxiously. YaLin paused and reluctantly met the gaze of eyes far older than their years.

"There were no Dreams, my father," he said gently and hurried into the hut before the next question could form.

"No Dreams?" The Old Dreamer followed his son inside. "You have always had Dreams. Did you not sleep well?"

YaLin seated himself on the packed dirt floor and called to his wife for breakfast. "I slept long and soundly, my father, but"—he smiled and shook his head—"there were no Dreams."

YaLin's wife moved slowly, serving the breakfast. She had not wanted to marry a Dreamer, though she liked YaLin well enough. "I would have a husband who lies at night with his wife and not alone in the desert," she had insisted stubbornly. But her parents, sensible of the honor done her, had forced the match. That YaLin did not spend all his nights in the desert was evidenced by the fact that she was now heavy with child. It was a son she carried—YaLin had Dreamed it.

Watching his wife as she moved awkwardly about her chores, YaLin wished that he could have had such simple Dreams the night before. A son for the Dreamer, a *tu* buck brought in by the hunters, the death of the old chief—these were the things a Dreamer should Dream. YaLin wondered if he were to be cursed as his father had been. And yet, even the Dreams of the Old Dreamer, however tragic, had been about known and knowable things. But the latest Dream of YaLin . . .

He turned abruptly to his father. "Tell me of the Great Flood," he commanded.

A spasm of pain crossed the Old Dreamer's face. He was reluctant to dredge up the ancient memories, but the wish of a Dreamer was not to be denied.

"I Dreamed it all. It has been many, many years, and I have tried to forget it, but the Dream stays with me always. I was young and strong, and my heart sang with the wind as I went through the days. I had a beautiful wife and two fine young sons, and the Dreams were good. And then I Dreamed the Flood.

"The People of Lith had lived in the Tuan Valley for longer than the longest memories could remember, and the river had always been our friend. But I Dreamed the Flood, and the river became our enemy. The rain fell on the valley as it has never fallen before or since. The crazed river ran wild through the village, destroying the homes and carrying off our people. I saw my own wife carried off by the rampaging waters and could do nothing to save her because I held our sons in my arms. One life lost to save two. She would have wished it so."

He paused, feeling anew the age-old and ageless grief.

"I told the Elders, of course, and we made plans to leave the valley, but it was too late. We had barely begun to plan when the rains came, and there was no time. No time. It was all as I had Dreamed."

The Old Dreamer sat silent for long moments. "It's a curse, my son," he said finally, his voice heavy with bitterness. "Our people think it a blessing, but it's a curse. The events foretold by the Dreams will come to pass, whether we wish it or not. Why Dream at all? If events will be as they will be, why must we suffer them twice? It is not just!"

YaLin shrugged and rose to his feet. "It is the will of the gods, my father."

He spent the day in the temple. But he was not praying. He was thinking. Was it really the will of the gods? Did the gods send the Dreams as a prophecy of what was to come?

Or did the Dreams come from the Dreamer himself?

If the Old Dreamer had never Dreamed the Flood, would there have been a Flood? YaLin's father believed that the events foretold by the Dreams could not be prevented. But there were legends, tales passed down from the Old Times, of Dreamers who had prevented their disastrous Dreams from being realized. The Dreamer had done it. Not the Chief, nor the Council of Elders, but the Dreamer.

YaLin knew that he must prevent this Dream from becoming fact. The People of Lith had suffered too much already. After the Great Flood, the Old Dreamer had not had to Dream the flight from the Tuan Valley. The tribe, such of it as had survived, had fled in terror from its ancient homeland to the distant prairies. But he had Dreamed the drought and famine that turned the grasslands to desert. And when the people had begun to reclaim the desert and to hope again, he had Dreamed the Plague. It had carried off his second wife, his baby daughter, and his very soul. He Dreamed no more. His eldest son, YaLin, scarcely out of childhood, had become the Young Dreamer. And the Dreams were good.

That night, after his day in the temple, YaLin stood with YuAng under the star-blazoned skies.

"You are troubled, my brother." It was statement. YuAng knew his brother well; YaLin could hide little from him.

"It is natural," the Young Dreamer replied. "I have always Dreamed when I have held vigil in the desert. Last night there were no Dreams. It is a troubling thing. But tonight there will be Dreams. I am sure of it."

"You will not tell me of last night's Dreams?"

"There were no Dreams!" A curt reply, intended to dismiss.

YuAng studied his older brother intently for a long moment. "Sleep well, Dreamer. May the Dreams of the night be good," he said formally, and turned back to the village.

Fire, death, and destruction. The village in flames and the screaming children fleeing into the desert to die, while their elders perished trying to save the village.

"No! It must not be! This thing shall not happen. I will not allow it!" The sleeping spirit of YaLin the Dreamer did violent battle with the Dream. But still it raged, with merciless intensity.

"Why?" The Young Dreamer writhed in agony. "Why must the tribe die? Why the pain and suffering? Why?"

Then, suddenly, cool and distant, came a reply. "You are mistaken. Your people will not die. There will be no death. No pain or suffering. We come in peace and friendship."

The Dream was gone. Instead there were only the vast dark reaches of space. YaLin floated through the tranquil void for immeasurable minutes before he dared ask, "Who are you? Where do you come from?"

"We are friends," the voice drifted back calmly. "We journey from a distant star to spread harmony through the universe. Who are you?"

"I am YaLin the Dreamer. In the name of the People of Lith I bid you welcome. When do you come?"

"Tomorrow. We come tomorrow. Down from the sky. Tomorrow, tomorrow . . ." and the Dream faded away.

YaLin awakened long before the first pale flecks of dawn lightened the sky. He lay marveling at what he had done. He had Dreamed a savage Dream telling of the very death throes of his people. And he had vanquished it with another Dream.

A wondrous Dream!

All day YaLin sat at the top of a hill outside the village, watching for he knew not what. He was alone because he had wished it so. The people knew the Dreams were good, and they were content to wait.

When YaLin saw the tiny speck in the distance descend to the ground, he knew it was what he awaited. He walked slowly and confidently across the desert to greet the mysterious visitors. By the time he came near the shining silver tower which had come down from the sky, a few of the visitors were already out of it, making their first cautious explorations. Ya-Lin, wrapped in the immense dignity of his office, approached the nearest man and greeted him ceremoniously.

They were strange, these creatures from another star. Strange not only in appearance, but in thought. They had been taught by their wise men that all thinking creatures in the universe must look much like themselves. And they believed it. So the man who killed YaLin did not even guess that the giant lizardlike creature suddenly towering over him was a Dreamer of the People of Lith, nor that its savage roar was a speech of welcome. He was only defending himself from a wild beast.

Dreamers were sacred to the People of Lith. The death of any other tribal member might have been forgiven as an understandable error. But the Dreamer was sacred, and the death of YaLin had to be avenged if it took the life of every other member of the tribe. And it did. It was war, quick and sharp and bitter. And when it was over, the last Dreams of the Young Dreamer YaLin, last Dreamer of the People of Lith, had come to pass.

EYE FOR AN EYE
Lloyd Biggle, Jr.

Walter Dudley and his wife paused at the top of the ramp for their first glimpse of the independent world of Maylor. The bleak landscape stretched unbroken to the taut line of the horizon. "It doesn't look very interesting," Dudley observed.

Eleanor Dudley was more emphatic. "It stinks."

"Maybe it'll be better in town," Dudley said, though he knew it wouldn't. One could not expect to find much of the tinsel of civilization on a world that was, admittedly, the last refuge of the failure.

A noisy, vilely malodorous groundcar arrived in a choking swirl of dust and fumes, and they climbed aboard with their hand luggage. Minutes later, bounced and jolted to the verge of nausea, they were deposited at the diminutive passenger terminal.

Hamal Bakr, the Galactic Insurance Company's temporary resident manager, met them at the terminal. Dudley disliked him at sight. Not only was he tall and handsome, but his casual afternoon robe displayed his trim figure with the effectiveness of a military uniform. Dudley had met his type before —met it frequently, and always to his profound regret. Bakr would be the darling of his sector manager, and even his infrequent failures would count more than other men's successes.

He crushed Dudley's hand and bent low over Eleanor's, brushing her fingers with his mustache and murmuring that this world of Maylor's long-standing reputation as the abode of beautiful women had been sheer fraud until the moment of her arrival. Eleanor tittered.

"I've found an apartment for you," Bakr said. "You won't like it, but it's the best I could do on short notice. There's a terrible housing shortage here."

"Whatever it is, we've probably seen worse," Dudley said. But he doubted that, too.

"I have my 'car waiting," Bakr said. "I'll drive you."

He herded them through customs, bullying officials, snarling at baggage attendants, and frightening porters. Then he loaded them and their luggage into his sleek groundcar and triumphantly roared away with them, trailing clouds of dust.

"In case you're in suspense," he said to Dudley, "I can summarize the present condition of our business in three words: There isn't any."

"I gathered that the situation wasn't healthy."

"It's worse than just unhealthy. It's deceased. If you're thinking of doing anything except arrange a decent burial, forget it."

"Strange," Dudley murmured. "What's the competition? I *know* no one has better air vehicular coverage than Galactic, and our fire coverages—"

"There aren't any air vehicles on Maylor. They're prohibited. Too dangerous. But this—" Bakr swerved, narrowly missing an oncoming 'car that crowded the center of the road. "This they consider safe."

"They must have an appalling accident rate. How many groundcar policies do we have in force?"

"One."

Dudley stared. "Just one policy? On the entire planet? You can't be serious!"

"But I am serious. The Galactic Insurance Company has one groundcar policy in force on this planet, and it's mine. I only bought it to be patriotic. Because of the peculiar customs and legalities of Maylor, its citizens consider insurance unnecessary or incomprehensible or both. They won't buy it at any premium or under any circumstances. Wasn't this explained to you? I thought you were being sent out to wind things up and close the office."

"Nothing was explained to me," Dudley said grimly. "I was sent out to make the business go here—or else."

"Old man, I had no idea, or I'd have broken the news gently."

Eleanor drawled, "Think nothing of it. This is Walter's ninth assignment in four years. You might say he's used to failing."

They drove on in silence.

The atmosphere of Maylor's capital city, when they finally reached it, was a nerve-shattering blend of dirt and noise and confusion. Factories vomited smoke, groundcar traffic was deafening, and the low buildings were hideous. Dudley appraised the shoddy frame dwelling with the eye of an insurance expert and shuddered.

"Fire insurance?"

"One policy in force," Bakr said. "Mine."

The architecture improved markedly as they approached the center of the city. Buildings were of brick, some of them two or three stories high. The traffic situation became increasingly disorganized. Pedestrians and vehicles shared the narrow street, the foot traffic usually, but not always, keeping to the sides. Buildings fronted directly on the street. It was possible to take a cautious step from a doorway and be struck by a groundcar.

"Hazards like this and no insurance?" Dudley asked incredulously.

Bakr did not answer.

Directly ahead of them, chaos swirled. Construction work was underway on one of the buildings. The workers and their equipment were scattered about in the street, and pedestrians and groundcars zestfully maneuvered among them.

"That's the place," Bakr said. "I might as well stop here." He edged to the side of the street, nudging pedestrians out of the way, and came to a stop almost grazing a building. "We'll get your stuff upstairs, and then I'll show you the office."

"What are they doing to the place?" Eleanor asked.

"They're adding another story."

"And we're supposed to live there with that racket on all sides?" she exclaimed.

"They only work during the day. It isn't a bad place, really. It's a luxury apartment, and it's within walking distance of the office—if you have the nerve to walk, that is. It could be a lot worse."

"I believe you," Dudley said.

Bakr and Dudley carried up the trunks and suitcases and left Eleanor fuming in the three cramped rooms that constituted a luxury apartment on the world of Maylor. Back in the street, Dudley paused to watch the construction workers.

A man was hauling on a slender rope, which fed through a complex of pulleys and slowly raised an enormous load of brick. Pedestrians strolled indifferently beneath the swaying load. Dudley turned away, genuinely frightened. "Don't they take any safety precautions at all?"

"Sure. There's another workman standing by in case the one with the rope gets tired. If you'd ask them, they'd say they very rarely have an accident."

"Liability insurance?"

"They don't even understand what it is," Bakr said. "When you have a chance, take a close look at that rope. The hemp is of poor quality, and the rope has only two strands. If one parted, the other couldn't hold the load. Shall we go?"

Dudley nodded, and they climbed into Bakr's 'car.

"They're a fine-looking people," Dudley observed. The Maylorites were a sturdy, blond race, handsome and cheerful. Smiles greeted them from all sides.

"They are that," Bakr agreed. "Maylor *is* the abode of beautiful women. Good-looking men, too. But they're much too virtuous for my taste."

The Maylor office of Galactic Insurance was a small third-story room. It contained a desk, two chairs, and a row of empty filing cabinets. Unopened cartons of policy, endorsement, and record forms were stacked in a corner.

"No staff?" Dudley asked.

"No work," Bakr said. "I fired the one employee the day I took over."

"How long have you been here?"

"Three months. I was on my way back to the home office for reassignment when the Maylor resident manager was fired, and McGivern asked me to hold the fort until he assigned a new one. I've been recommending twice a week that the office be closed. I was afraid McGivern might promote me and give me the job. You have my sympathy, but there isn't much else I can do for you."

"You can fill me in on the situation. I understand that this office did very well when it was first opened."

"Business was sensational. Galactic was the first insurance company on Maylor. Now it's the last. A couple of hundred others have come and gone."

"Stubbornness has made Galactic great," Dudley murmured.

"That's home office propaganda, and you know it. Stubbornness doesn't accomplish a thing on Maylor except to lose money. Business was sensational for the first six months. Then the claims started to come in, and in another six months the only policies in force were those of Galactic's employees."

"What happened? Were the claims rejected?"

Bakr shook his head. "A native holding a fire insurance policy had a fire. The company offered a generous settlement, but he wouldn't accept it. He demanded—and got—his premium refunded. Then he proceeded to scream long and loudly that Galactic's insurance was no good."

"If we offered to pay the claim, I don't understand why—"

"He'd insured himself against fire, and he had a fire anyway. Why carry fire insurance if it doesn't keep you from having fires?"

"But surely if the principles of insurance were properly explained—"

"Not on Maylor. People here don't want money. They want to not have fires. Same thing happened with life insurance. A native insured his life with Galactic, and he died anyway. Clearly the insurance policy wasn't worth the paper it was printed on, and the offer of money in the face of such an obvious failure constituted a form of bribery. I could go on and on. When a native of Maylor insures his life, he expects not to die. When he insures his groundcar against accidents, he expects not to have accidents. If the insurance won't keep him from dying or from having accidents or from anything else it claims to insure him against, why carry insurance? There are perfectly sound reasons for this attitude. You can study the legal and social and historical backgrounds if you like—you *will* study them—but all you'll get out of it will be a slightly better understanding of why you can't sell insurance."

"I see," Dudley said.

"I'm leaving on the next ship. I'd suggest that you come along."

"I can't do that. I've had some miserable luck, and I've been relieved of my last eight assignments, but I've never quit. And McGivern—"

Dudley shrugged morosely. The mere recollection of that last interview with McGivern was enough to cost him a night's sleep.

"Damn McGivern," Bakr said. "Damn Galactic, if it holds you responsible for things beyond your control. There are other insurance companies."

"Which don't hire failures. Not in positions of responsibility."

"Did McGivern give you a time limit?"

"Three months, which means nothing at all. Once he gave me six months, and then he showed up on the *Indemnity* when I'd only been on the job for two weeks, hung around for a couple of days looking over my shoulder, and relieved me. It wouldn't surprise me if he turned up tomorrow wanting to know why the problem isn't solved yet."

Bakr got to his feet. "That's what can happen when the boss has his own private space yacht. Well, you know what you're up against. Any help I can give you in the next seven days you're welcome to."

"I'll need a groundcar, I suppose."

"You can rent one. I'll take care of it for you."

"And insurance on it."

Bakr grinned. "Certainly. Fire insurance on your personal property, too. Liability, accident, theft, health—write yourself a batch of policies. You can double Galactic's business your first day on the job. When I leave, I'll be canceling my policies, but for a week you'll have a sensational record."

From the room's one window Dudley watched him drive away. At the corner his car brushed the robe of a woman pedestrian, and she halted in the midst of traffic to smile after him sweetly. Shaking his head, Dudley retreated to the desk.

He had three months—maybe. He had no advertising budget and wouldn't have one until he produced a volume of business to support it. Within those limitations he had to contrive nothing less than a massive campaign to educate the people of Maylor to the value of insurance.

Personal salesmanship was the only answer, and he'd have to apply it quickly—pinpoint the area of most obvious need, devise a dramatic gimmick to catch people's attention, and hammer away with it. He could begin by tabulating recent losses. A rash of fires always put the public in a wonderfully receptive state of mind for fire insurance, and a series of break ins never failed to soften a merchant's resistance to theft insurance.

He walked down the three flights of stairs to the general store that occupied the ground floor of the building and asked the clerk where he could buy a newspaper.

"I'm sorry, sir," the young man said. "We have none left."

"Is there someone else who'd have one?"

"I very much doubt it, sir. It's been out more than a week, you see."

"When will the next issue be available?"

The clerk looked surprised. "Why—not until next month!"

"Thank you."

Dudley introduced himself, and the clerk said blankly, "Galactic—*Insurance?* Oh, Galactic. You're upstairs."

Dudley agreed that when he was in his office he was upstairs. "Has this neighborhood been troubled by burglaries lately?" he asked.

"Burglaries? What is that?"

"Thefts, stealing—"

The clerk pondered this. "I'll ask," he said finally. He entered an office at the rear of the store. Through the open door Dudley watched him converse guardedly with an older man. A moment later the two of them bent over a book, the older man energetically flipping pages. Dudley moved closer and managed to identify the book. It was a dictionary.

The clerk returned and shook his head apologetically. "No, sir. We've never had anything like that."

On his way out Dudley verified what he'd thought was a faulty observation when he entered. The store's street door had no lock. Neither were there locks on the entrances to the adjoining stores. Neither, now that he thought about it, was there a lock on the door of his office.

No insurance company managed by sane men would underwrite theft insurance on a business establishment that had no lock on its door, but the clerk claimed there were no losses by theft. He did not even know what the word meant!

Dudley dropped the subject of theft insurance and went back to his office to stand at the window and meditate on the perilous groundcar traffic.

Bakr returned, settled himself comfortably in the desk

chair, and announced that Dudley's groundcar would be available in a couple of days. "That's fast service for Maylor," he said.

"I'll need lessons," Dudley said. "I've never driven one before."

"That needn't worry you. The natives don't know how to drive, either."

"Even so—"

"Right. I'll supervise your instruction myself. It'll give me something to do. And tonight I want you and Eleanor to be my guests for dinner. Afterward I'll take you on a comprehensive tour of Maylor City's night life. About twenty minutes will do the job. Is there anything else I can do for you?"

"I'd like to see a newspaper."

Bakr scowled. "That *is* a problem. The thing only publishes once a month. I'll try to dig one up."

"I've never heard of a city of this size without a daily paper. Is there a shortage of newsprint?"

"There's a shortage of news. Nothing happens on Maylor."

"What about advertising?"

"It's limited to disgustingly polite announcements. 'Thomas Peawinkle and Son are pleased to announce that they will have no imported shoes for sale until the next consignment arrives.' That sort of thing."

"I'm beginning to understand why you call the situation impossible."

"My friend, even now you have absolutely no idea as to how impossible it is!"

"I'll have to do some thinking."

"If you're a religious man, you might pray for divine guidance. That's the only thing that's likely to help. I'll call for you and Eleanor at seven."

He left Dudley to his despondent window gazing.

The restaurant was so spotlessly clean and so starkly unadorned that Dudley was reminded of a hospital ward. The young waitresses had a rosy, freshly scrubbed appearance.

" 'Bland' is the word for it," Bakr said. "Everything and everybody on Maylor is bland. That includes the food."

"It smells delicious," Eleanor remarked as a waitress moved gracefully past their table with a steaming tray.

"Wait'll you taste it. I come forearmed, though, and you're welcome to share." Bakr placed a small flask on the table in front of him.

"What is it?" Eleanor asked.

"Sauce. It's a special blend mixed to my specifications. It's hot. Most people think it blisters their mouths, but that's the way I like it."

He unscrewed the cap and passed the flask to Eleanor, who sniffed cautiously. "It smells—interesting."

She handed it to Dudley, and one quick whiff brought tears to his eyes. "Whew—do you *eat* this stuff?"

Bakr laughed. "If *you* think it's strong, you should see how the natives react to it. For all their sturdy appearance, every one of them has a weak stomach. I suppose that accounts for the bland food."

Their order arrived, a thick, creamy stew with large dumplings floating in it. Bakr applied his custom-made sauce with gusto. Dudley tasted the food, grimaced, and agreed that it lacked something.

"The commissary out at the port has some imported spices and sauces," Bakr said. "I should have told you to stock up. You can't buy such things anywhere else. Try a little of this."

Eleanor added a light dash of Bakr's sauce and praised the result enthusiastically. Dudley took the flask, miscalculated as he tilted it, and spilled a gush of sauce into his bowl. He regarded it with dismay as it stained the food an unappetizing brown.

"Clumsy!" Eleanor snapped.

Dudley shrugged, stirred the stew, tasted it. Instantly he doubled up, eyes watering, choking, gasping for breath, while Bakr pounded him on the back.

"You put twice as much on!" he said accusingly to Bakr.

"But I'm used to the stuff," Bakr said. "And I like it. You'd better reorder and try again."

Dudley reordered, but he flatly refused a second offer of the sauce. He ate glumly and finished his meal in silence. Eleanor mockingly added more sauce to her food and devoted her full attention to Bakr.

"Now, then," Bakr said when they had finished eating. "A night spot or two. Some dancing such as you've never seen before, where the partners exchange affectionate glances from across the room. Singing to a weird musical scale that approximates a banshee's howling. Comedians who have contests to see who can tell the most pointless story, and the more pointless it is, the louder the natives laugh. Nonalcoholic liquor that tastes like water laced with extract of onion. Maylorian night life is about as wide-open as a prison camp, but you might as well sample it now and see what you're in for."

"No, thank you," Dudley said. "I want to work on this insurance problem."

"I vote for the night life," Eleanor said.

Dudley glared at her.

"We'll drop Walter at the apartment," Eleanor told Bakr. "He works better when I'm not around."

"I can understand that," Bakr said.

Bakr stopped his 'car at the apartment entrance, and Dudley walked away without a backward glance. His anger at Eleanor's transgressions had long since dulled to indifference. He was thinking, rather, about McGivern. How would McGivern go about selling insurance to the citizens of Maylor? Better—how would McGivern expect Dudley to proceed?

He made himself comfortable on the narrow sofa, his inhalator at his elbow, and confronted the problem through fragrant puffs of smoke. His objective, as he saw it, was to condition the natives to think of personal injury or property loss in monetary terms. Once they grasped the concept of financial compensation, their awareness of the need for insurance would follow inevitably. One claim, properly settled, would establish a precedent; two would set a pattern.

But how could he properly settle a claim if there was no insurance in force?

He dug Galactic's *Underwriting Handbook* from a suitcase and began listing endorsements to standard policy forms that might make them more suitable to the world of Maylor. He found so few that seemed appropriate that he began to draw up his own endorsements. When Bakr and Eleanor finally returned, potently trailing alcoholic fumes, the floor of the small living room was littered with paper and Dudley was nursing a headache.

"I thought there was no alcohol on Maylor," he said sourly.

"Officially there isn't," Bakr said. "It does such appalling things to those delicate Maylorian stomachs that it's banned as a poison. Fortunately the Maylorites are such innocent, trusting souls that smuggling is child's play. I brought my private stock with me. How are you making out?"

"I'm not," Dudley admitted.

"You'll have to face the facts, Old Man. Insurance and the Maylorites are absolutely incompatible. They're a disgustingly ethical race. They not only don't want something for nothing, but they positively refuse to accept it. They're also disgustingly well-balanced. There isn't a psychiatrist on Maylor—or a mental hospital. They aren't afraid of the future, or of fate, or of the so-called 'acts of God.' They aren't even superstitious. Take away greed and fear, and what motives do you have left for buying insurance?"

"So we're back to lesson number one in the sales manual," Dudley mused. "Motivation. If the old stand-bys won't work, we'll have to think up some new motives."

"*You'll* have to think them up, Old Man. I resigned from thinking about the Maylor situation a long time ago. Naturally I wish you luck, and if I can help in any way except by thinking, let me know."

For the next two days Dudley spent most of his waking moments in futile thinking. He thought lying on the sofa, hands clapped to his ears to filter out some of the racket caused by the construction work going on just above his head. He thought leaning from the window, watching the tangle of traffic in the street below and waiting with bated breath for a load of brick to snap the slender rope and crush an innocent passer-by. The load passed his window, and on one ascent he noticed that it bumped the side of the building frequently, and that the bumping had frayed the rope sling on all four sides. If one strand parted—he turned away shaking his head. No conscientious insurance underwriter would accept coverage on such a risk, and yet he would have to do so if he wanted to sell insurance on Maylor. There were no better risks.

When he tired of the apartment, he went to the Galactic office and spent tedious hours contemplating the lockless door. Bakr helped tremendously by entertaining Eleanor, but by the end of that second day she was complaining that she had seen all of Maylor City that she wanted or intended to see.

On the third day Dudley's rented groundcar was delivered, and Dudley and Bakr took it out for a driving lesson. Dudley drove slowly, horrified at the risks taken by the nonchalant pedestrians, and Bakr chuckled repeatedly at his discomfiture.

"How are you doing with the insurance situation?" Bakr asked.

"I haven't been able to come up with anything," Dudley confessed. "If I could manage a proper settlement of just one claim, I'd have a strong selling point to work with. But how can I settle a claim if there's no insurance in force?"

"One claim," Bakr said thoughtfully. "Yes, a claim would be a help—if you could talk the claimant into *being* a claimant."

They had turned into a quiet residential section, and the 'car was bouncing wildly on the irregular cobblestones. "One claim," Bakr said again. "You have insurance on yourself, don't you? Didn't you write a liability policy on this groundcar?"

"Of course. But a claim involving myself—"

"A claim is a claim, no matter whom it involves. And"— Bakr grabbed at the steering wheel—"here it is!"

The 'car veered crazily. A woman screamed, and Dudley frantically dug at the brake pedal. He brought the 'car to a halt inches short of a flimsy wood dwelling and leaped out to bend over the young woman who lay pinned under it.

"Why didn't you use your brake?" Bakr hissed. "You've killed her!"

Dudley turned his back on the crushed body, valiantly trying not to be sick. "Is she dead?"

"They don't come any deader," Bakr said grimly. "Look. I'll have to get to Eleanor right away. Hide her somewhere."

"Eleanor?"

"Leave it to me. I'll take care of it."

He pushed through the gathering crowd of spectators and broke into a run. Dudley leaned against the car and miserably contemplated the still body.

A young doctor arrived from somewhere. With the help of the spectators he pulled the body from under the 'car, clucked his tongue sadly, and sacrificed his white robe to cover her. Three police officers trotted up looking ridiculously gay in their checkered robes. One took charge of the situation and sent the other two hurrying off on urgent errands. He accepted Dudley's identification and recorded the information on a report form. The crowd of spectators continued to grow. Dudley searched the circle of faces for indications of the indignation he expected, and to his intense surprise he found them regarding him with polite sympathy.

The police officer patted him on the shoulder. "The judge should be here soon."

"*Judge?*" Dudley breathed.

"Why don't you wait in the 'car?"

Dudley swallowed his protest and staggered to the 'car. His knees had been on the verge of collapse since he first saw the woman's body. He eased himself into the rear seat and waited, and soon the woman's husband appeared, escorted by a police officer, and the judge arrived from the opposite direction in a flurry of scarlet robes. The husband, a sturdy, honest-looking young man in a tradesman's robe, bent resignedly over his dead wife and then quietly stepped aside. The judge, a robust old man with formidably sagging jowls, studied Dudley's papers with a scowl.

"An Alien! Now we shall have all manner of tiresome complications. Have you a wife, Alien Dudley?"

"Certainly," Dudley said.

"You have a wife but no manners at all!" the judge snapped.

"You must stand before the judge," the police officer whispered.

Dudley scrambled from the car and faced the judge.

"And you must say, 'Your Wisdom,' when you answer," the police officer whispered.

"Now, then," the judge said. "It would be entirely too much to expect that your wife would be here on Maylor. Where is she?"

"Here on Maylor," Dudley said, belatedly remembering to add, "Your Wisdom."

"Excellent!" The judge's glum expression vanished. He flashed a plump smile at Dudley and examined the papers again. "Then we can settle this matter before lunch. Is your wife at this address?"

"She was there when I left this morning, Your Wisdom."

"Excellent!"

"Do you wish for her to be brought here, Your Wisdom?" the police officer asked.

"We shall go there. At once."

"In the violator's 'car, Your Wisdom?"

"Of course. Otherwise, I shall be late for lunch."

Dudley rode in the rear seat with the bereaved husband; the judge rode in front beside the police officer, who drove. Dudley uneasily watched the husband, who had not spoken. If the young man was not dazed by shock, his composure was truly heroic.

Dudley turned away and sought to convince himself that he had nothing to worry about. He had insurance—very good insurance. He said, "Your—Wisdom?"

The judge turned.

"I have insurance, Your Wisdom."

The judge considered this. "What is insurance?" he asked.

"It's—well—it's insurance, you see, and when there's an accident—"

He broke off lamely. The judge had returned his attention to the clutter of traffic that surrounded them. They continued the trip in silence.

The police officer parked the 'car a short distance from the apartment entrance, and they moved toward it in single file, Dudley making a cautious circuit of the area beneath an ascending load of brick. The judge stoically marched straight ahead.

They climbed the stairs. Dudley opened the door of the apartment—which, like his office, had no lock—and called, "Eleanor!"

There was no answer. The apartment was empty. Dudley examined the luggage and noted that a suitcase was missing.

"She isn't here, Your Wisdom," he told the judge.

"Indeed. She is visiting a neighbor, perhaps? Or gone purchasing?"

"I guess she's just—gone. She took a suitcase."

"Indeed." The judge seated himself on the sofa and looked at Dudley severely. "It seems that I shall after all be late for lunch." He nodded at the police officer. "You will make inquiries. At once."

"Yes, Your Wisdom."

"And you." The judge pointed at Dudley. "I warn you. If

this case is not settled promptly, I intend to charge my maximum fee."

"I don't mind paying your maximum fee, Your Wisdom," Dudley said. "I don't really see what Eleanor has to do with this. After all, I *do* have insurance."

"Eleanor is your wife's name? She has everything to do with it. On this world we follow the Rule of Justice."

"But my insurance—"

"You have deprived this man of his wife. You must give him your wife. If he is willing to accept her, that is. It is only simple justice."

"Eleanor might not consent to that," Dudley protested.

"She has no choice in the matter."

"But my insurance—"

"What *is* this insurance?"

"It will pay him a cash settlement for his loss, Your Wisdom."

"Cash!" the judge screamed. "You would substitute money for justice? What barbarous customs you aliens have!"

The return of the police officer saved him from the attack of apoplexy that seemed imminent. The two conferred in whispers, and the judge's expression gradually changed from one of anger to amazement. "A conspiracy?" he demanded.

"It would appear so, Your Wisdom."

"But the Alien Dudley could not have warned his wife. He did not even know our Rule of Justice."

"The fact remains, Your Wisdom—"

"True. The fact remains. And if the Alien Dudley is involved in the conspiracy, I shall be harsh with him. What are we to do with him in the meantime, if I am not to miss my lunch altogether?"

"I don't know, Your Wisdom."

"You should know. Justice is your profession, too. We must incarcerate him. That is the Rule—incarceration after the event and before the judgment. The question is, where? In all of my judicial experience such a thing has never happened. Do you have any knowledge of a judge incarcerating a violator?"

"No, Your Wisdom."

"We once had special places of incarceration, but because of our present commendable efficiency in applying the Rule of Justice, they are no longer needed. Several legal histories mention them. They don't assist us in the present dilemma, however. I leave the entire problem in your hands, officer. Incarcerate the violator!"

"Yes, Your Wisdom."

"And continue your search for the wife, of course. For the next three hours I shall be at lunch."

After a lengthy conference with his colleagues, the police officer decided to incarcerate Dudley in his own apartment. The only other place available, it seemed, was his own home, and he saw no reason to take a violator into his home when the violator had a home of his own to be incarcerated in.

"You must not leave until the judge orders your release," the police officer said. He left, taking the bereaved husband with him, and Dudley found himself officially incarcerated by an unlocked door. The remainder of the day he paced the small apartment, counted the bricks that were hoisted past his window, cursed Hamal Bakr as a murderer wholly devoid of conscience and, when he could concentrate, gave fleeting thought to the insurance problem.

What Maylor needed, he decided, was an entirely different concept of the insurance claim settlement: a type of barter arrangement, where the insurance company restored a loss without reference to money. It would create endless complications, and it would require the training of an entirely new breed of claim adjuster; but he thought he could, given sufficient time, develop claim procedures that would meet the requirements of Maylor's strange Rule of Justice.

Thaddeus McGivern was not in the habit of allowing anyone sufficient time for anything. The plaque on his office wall read, "RESULTS—*NOW!*"

The police officer called again the next day—not to see if Dudley had escaped his incarceration, which possibility would not even occur to him, but to see if Eleanor had returned.

"The judge is becoming impatient," he announced. "I apologize for the reflection on your honesty, but he has asked me to determine if you are hiding your wife."

"Certainly not," Dudley said. "Eleanor isn't the kind of wife one would hide when there's a good chance of getting rid of her. I haven't the vaguest notion of where she is. Unless—you might ask an alien named Hamal Bakr. He probably knows."

"We have asked Alien Bakr. He says he does not know."

"Did you search his apartment?"

"What would be the point of that when he has said she is not there?"

"I have a feeling," Dudley said, "that this is going to be a long incarceration."

The following morning Dudley was awakened by a violent pounding on his door. Sleepily he stumbled to open it, and the enraged apparition that greeted him shocked him into instant, terrified wakefulness. "McGivern!" he gasped.

The apparition remained—as large as life and several degrees angrier. McGivern's purple suit was immaculate, but he'd crushed his hat in his hand. He pointed with it. "Dudley!" he bellowed. "Why aren't you at the office?"

"Where did you—I mean, how—"

"I just arrived. On the *Indemnity,* of course, and my first stop was the Galactic office to see how my special trouble-shooter was proceeding with the revitalization of our business on this planet. I'll be interested in hearing about this new technique that enables you to sell insurance while in bed."

"There's been some trouble," Dudley said lamely.

"Nonsense! Get dressed, man, and come along. There's *work* to do!"

"I can't come," Dudley said. "I've been—well—arrested."

"Arrested? Have you let this bunch of hicks—" McGivern waddled across the room and sank his weight into the protesting sofa. "I've been patient with you, Dudley; far too patient, but I've reached the end. You won't learn. You have enough ability to fill even my shoes, someday, but you lack gumption, and without gumption your ability isn't worth a damn. What sort of trouble?"

"It's rather complicated."

"I'll bet it is. You're under house arrest, I take it." He scratched fretfully at the polished dome of his bald head. "I'd hate to let you go, Dudley, but you just won't learn. Take that situation on Himil. All you had to do was bribe a few legislators, and you funked it."

"I thought I could find an honest way—"

"Dudley, we are not moralists or philosophers. We're practical businessmen." He pointed his hat again. "Be *ruthless,* Dudley. Chart your objective, and smash anyone that gets in the way. You aren't playing school games, now—you don't give back the marbles you win at the end of the day. Here's an entire planet without insurance. It's an opportunity to make any ambitious resident manager drool. What have you done about it?"

"I've worked out a plan for an entirely new—"

"Bah! What have you *done?* Galactic can't pay stockholders' dividends with plans." He struggled out of the cavity in the sofa and thrust a fistful of money at Dudley. "Here—fix this arrest thing. I'm going to nose around and get the feel of the situation."

"I don't think—"

"Good. You've been spending entirely too much time thinking. Stop it, and start *doing* a few things. The hotels in this town stink, so I'll be staying on the *Indemnity.* As soon as you've fixed the police, report there. I can't give you more than a couple of days, Dudley. If you aren't straightened out by then, you're through."

He left Dudley nervously fingering the bribery money.

Dudley spent the remainder of the day alternately pondering the insurance problem and wondering what the police officer would do if he left the apartment. He had no intention of offering a bribe, either to the police or to the judge; but he knew he had to do one thing promptly: locate Eleanor. She would never allow herself to be ordered into a marriage, but if she were found, the police would have no further claim on Dudley. Their problem would be with Eleanor, and they were welcome to it.

He doubted, though, that he'd be able to turn her over to the police even if he did locate her. She was not to blame for Bakr's muddling attempt to create an insurance claim.

He could not be ruthless.

Dudley went to bed early that night, and he slept very badly.

The next morning the police officer came with the startling news that Eleanor had surrendered voluntarily. Her marriage to the dead woman's husband had been recorded, and Dudley's incarceration was terminated. The judge would, when he got around to it, bill Dudley for his fee.

"Am I divorced—legally separated—from Eleanor?" Dudley demanded.

"Certainly not! What if her new husband should divorce her? Just because you have deprived that man of his wife is no reason for your wife to be deprived of a husband. In order to be separated from her, you would have to divorce her yourself."

"Thank you for explaining it so clearly," Dudley said.

He drove his groundcar to the spaceport. McGivern's yacht, the *Indemnity,* was parked in a choice location near the terminal building where a sign said, "No Landing Permitted in This Area." McGivern was having breakfast. His temper had not improved since the previous day. The steward set a place for Dudley, and McGivern said, snarling around a mouthful of toast, "I've been up all night. Did you know hat this crummy planet doesn't even have an underworld?"

"No," Dudley said, "but it doesn't surprise me."

"All I need is an arsonist and a few thieves. With organization, they could create an overwhelming need for insurance within a week." He raised a steaming cup of beverage to his lips and slammed it down again. "Nothing. I can import them, of course, but I'd much prefer to patronize the local underworld. What do you have?"

"What is needed," Dudley said, "is an entirely different concept of claim settlement: A type of barter arrangement that would replace a lost object without reference to money. For example, where the liability insuring clause reads, 'The Company will pay in behalf of the insured,' we could change it to read, t'the Company will *furnish* in behalf of the insured.' "

"I don't like it," McGivern said. "These people are basically no different from people anywhere. Get them accustomed to the idea, and they'll gladly take money. You won't be able to stop them. But I agree that there are two aspects to this problem. The fire rate is unbelievably low. There aren't any thefts at all. There are hardly any groundcar accidents, and that isn't just unbelievable, it's impossible. We'll have to bring about enough losses to make insurance necessary, and we'll have to establish a precedent or two for settling losses with money. You take the second one. I'll look in on you tomorrow and see what you've done with it."

"I still think we should hire a local attorney to draw up new insurance policies to conform with local practices."

"There aren't any attorneys on Maylor," McGivern snapped. "I looked into that the first thing—which is what you should have done. Get a move on and find me that claim precedent."

Late the next morning Dudley sat at his desk in the Galactic office, nervously contemplating a blank sheet of paper. He'd been up all night, and the blank piece of paper was the same one he'd started with the previous evening. He leaped to his feet in panic when the door opened, but it wasn't McGivern—it was Hamal Bakr.

"Come home, Old Man," Bakr said with a grin. "All is forgiven. Eleanor has lunch waiting."

"What are you talking about?" Dudley demanded. "Eleanor just married—"

"Her new husband divorced her this morning."

"It didn't take him long to get acquainted with her."

"Oh, he didn't *want* to divorce her. He couldn't help himself."

"Eleanor frequently affects people that way."

"Nonsense. Have you looked into the divorce laws on Maylor? You should. If a husband refuses to eat the food his wife prepares, that's grounds for divorce. Eleanor fixed the guy's breakfast yesterday morning, right after the marriage ceremony. She laced it with that special sauce of mine. The guy got sick and had to be pumped out. For lunch she gave him more of the same, and his sensitive Maylorian stomach put him in the hospital overnight. This morning he refused to eat, and she called in a judge and got her divorce."

"Obviously some woman thought up that law."

"Could be. A man can divorce his wife any time he likes, just by refusing to eat, but there's no divorce unless she makes the complaint herself and proves there's nothing wrong with the food by eating it herself. Fortunately Eleanor has developed a taste for my sauce. It solved the problem neatly."

"Very neatly," Dudley agreed. "Have you seen McGivern?"

"Saw him yesterday. He gave me my new assignment— resident manager on Nunquad. It's a pushover, and I leave tonight as planned. Now come to lunch."

They walked back to the apartment, Dudley maintaining a glum, meditative silence, and Bakr cheerfully commenting on Maylorian social customs and several times plucking Dudley bodily from the menacing traffic. Eleanor met them at the apartment door, kissed Dudley gushily, and escorted him to the luncheon table.

"Maylorian stew," she said brightly. "The recipe was the property of the deceased wife of my late husband."

"Too bad she didn't take it with her," Dudley muttered. He poked doubtfully with his spoon, took a small amount to sample—and doubled up in agony.

"You put that sauce in it!" he exclaimed, when he had rinsed out his mouth and wiped his eyes.

"Delicious, isn't it?" Eleanor said. "Have some more."

"I can't eat the stuff, and you know it."

"This is a terrible blow to a woman's pride," Eleanor said. She went to the apartment door and opened it. The old judge stood there scowling.

"At lunchtime, too," he grumbled. "You Aliens have no innate sense of decency."

"Your Wisdom," Eleanor said, "my husband refuses to eat the food I have prepared."

"Is this true?" the judge demanded. "I ask you now, in the presence of a witness, to eat."

Dudley glared at Eleanor. He clenched his teeth and firmly shook his head.

"You will now eat of the food to demonstrate that it is properly prepared," the judge said to Eleanor.

"Certainly," Eleanor said. She took Dudley's bowl and ate noisily. "Delicious stuff," she said.

"The witness will note that the husband has refused to eat and that the wife has eaten. Present yourself at my office with your witness, and I shall draw up your Bill of Divorcement."

"Certainly, Your Wisdom," Eleanor said. "Shall we come now?"

"After lunch," the judge said. "That'll be in about three hours."

He went out, banging the door behind him.

"I still have some packing to do," Eleanor said. She flitted into the bedroom.

"I suppose Eleanor is leaving Maylor with you," Dudley said to Bakr.

Bakr nodded. "The ship leaves at midnight. We'll have the captain marry us as soon as we go on board."

"You're entirely welcome," Dudley said.

"Glad you feel that way, Old Man—though I can't understand why you're so eager to give up a wife like Eleanor. She was afraid you'd fight it."

"She flatters herself."

"At least we can part friends. And we wish you luck with the insurance problem and especially with McGivern. I've never seen the old boy in such a violent mood. It's too bad we didn't think of that divorce gimmick earlier. We could have saved a lot of trouble."

"Bakr!" Dudley exclaimed. "You killed that woman deliberately!"

"So what?" Bakr said with a grin. "Have you worked for McGivern all these years without his sermon getting through to you? Hasn't he ever pointed his finger and said, "Be ruthless!""

"He has. Quite recently, in fact."

"You should have listened. Men at the home office have been wondering for years when their bright boy Dudley will grow up and start doing a man's work. The groundcar accident was Eleanor's idea. She wanted to get you incarcerated so you couldn't keep her from leaving Maylor. Apart from divorce, the law on this planet is entirely on the husband's side. But neither of us bore you any ill will, and when we thought of that divorce gimmick, we used it to get the dead woman's husband out of your hair. We didn't have to, you know. I could have smuggled Eleanor away from Maylor and left you incarcerated indefinitely. Ready, Eleanor?"

"Ready," Eleanor said, bringing two suitcases from the bedroom. "You can junk the rest of the stuff, Walter, unless you want to keep it as a memento. Bye-bye. Keep a grip on yourself and don't be *too* ruthless."

Dudley went to the window and looked out. He saw Bakr and Eleanor leave the building together and walk slowly through the construction area. There was a momentary lull in the street traffic; the two of them were alone except for the workers, who were raising another load of bricks.

The impulse struck Dudley so suddenly, the timing was so perfect, that he acted before he quite knew what he was doing. He whipped his penknife from his pocket, leaned out, sliced the nearest strand of rope. The sling collapsed instantly and the entire load of bricks poured down upon Bakr and Eleanor.

The horrified workers ran forward. Dudley turned away, seated himself on the sofa, and waited. His only thought was that the still form under his groundcar had somehow been revenged, and he almost looked forward to suffering whatever penalty this queer Maylorian legal system imposed for killing one's own ex-wife.

Then McGivern burst into the room. "You idiot!" he panted. "Have you lost your mind?"

Dudley smiled calmly. "No opinion—except that I've never felt saner."

"I was across the street—saw the whole thing." McGivern flopped down beside him. "Don't blame you for getting rid of that alley cat, but—in broad daylight, with fifty witnesses about? There's bound to be a scandal, your connection with Galactic will be publicized, and it'll be bad for business. Had you thought about that?"

"I hadn't thought of it in precisely that way."

"You wouldn't. Consider yourself fired as of yesterday. If you can manage this so Galactic isn't mentioned, I'll furnish any money you need for your defense and buy you a one-way ticket to a place of your choice when—and if—they let you go."

"That's magnanimous of you."

"*I* think so. Why did you have to kill Bakr, too? I'll admit he wasn't much more than an ornament, but he had his uses. Of all the stupid, asinine, irrational things to do—"

There was a knock at the door. Dudley calmly admitted a police officer.

"There's been a most unfortunate accident," the officer said.

"*Accident!*" McGivern exclaimed.

The police officer looked at him doubtfully. "Which of you is the Alien Dudley?" Dudley nodded gravely. "A clumsy oaf of a workman has managed to kill your wife," the officer said. "Would you oblige us by identifying the body?"

"Is that necessary?" Dudley asked.

"No. Two of your neighbors have already done so. I have sent for a judge and the workman's wife."

"The *workman's* wife?" McGivern sputtered. "What the devil for?"

"The workman has killed Alien Dudley's wife. He must, therefore, give his wife to Alien Dudley. Are you not familiar with our Rule of Justice?"

For one of the few times in his life, McGivern was speechless.

"I shall return when all is ready for the marriage ceremony," the police officer said.

"Thank you," Dudley told him.

He returned to the window. A crowd of spectators had blocked off the street. Workmen were reloading the bricks, and a doctor's robe was spread over the two bodies.

"*Marriage ceremony!*" McGivern said hoarsely. "What are you up to?"

"Does it matter? You just fired me."

McGivern was silent for a long time. Finally he said, "Does this fiasco have anything to do with the insurance problem?"

"Certainly," Dudley told him. "What did you think I was working on?"

He intended the words as vicious sarcasm, but even as he spoke them, he realized that the situation placed the insurance problem in an entirely new light. In all of their previous claims they had been in the awkward position of offering a financial settlement to a claimant who didn't want it. Supposing the claimant demanded such a settlement?

He paced the floor energetically, while a strangely subdued McGivern looked on. "Can I help?" McGivern asked.

Dudley shook his head. "It's a long shot."

"I like men who play long shots. I like them even better when they win."

Another knock sounded, and Dudley admitted the police officer, a young judge, and an attractive young Maylorian woman.

"Alien Dudley?" the judge asked. "Are you ready for the ceremony?"

"I'm not completely familiar with your customs, Your Wisdom," Dudley said. "This procedure seems very strange to me. Where I come from, the custom is for the violator to pay financial compensation."

"Such a thing is unheard of on Maylor," the judge said. "How could money compensate for the loss of a wife?"

"Nevertheless, Your Wisdom, I would like to know if I cannot request compensation according to my own custom."

The judge frowned. "I don't know. I can't recall such a thing ever happening."

EYE FOR AN EYE   229

"Is there any law that would forbid such a thing, Your Wisdom?"

The police officer was regarding Dudley with open-mouthed amazement. The young woman modestly kept her eyes on the floor, as though the conversation could not possibly concern her. The judge had his eyes closed in thought.

"The rule requires only that justice be done," the judge announced finally. "I should have to consider whether or not it would be unjust to deny you justice according to your own custom. To my knowledge no such request has ever been made of a violator, but if such a request were made, I should—yes, I should feel obliged to honor it. Do you now make this request?"

"I do, Your Wisdom."

"What amount of compensation do you request?"

"Your Wisdom should establish the amount."

"That would require much thought on my part. There is no precedent; none at all. I shall have to postpone settlement of this case until I am able to reach a decision as to the amount."

"That will be satisfactory, Your Wisdom."

They filed out solemnly. Dudley closed the door and turned to find himself the recipient of one of McGivern's rare smiles. "Dudley, I badly underestimated you. This is the most brilliant stroke I've ever seen." McGivern scrambled to his feet and waddled about the room excitedly. "And *I* was telling *you* to be ruthless! You've wrapped the whole thing up nicely. This gives us our legal precedent. One more case—"

"We have it," Dudley said. "My groundcar killed a woman a few days ago. The husband—it's rather complicated —the husband ended up with nothing. Now I'll offer him a cash settlement, the amount to be determined by the judge. He'll refuse, but I'll tell him my own customs demand that I give it to him, and I'm sure he'll accept it just to oblige me. The Maylorites are a very obliging people."

"Well done, my boy. *Well done!*"

"And what progress have you made with *your* problem?"

McGivern started. "That's what I came to see you about. These people are so naive that hiring professional underworld men would be a waste of money. I took a few crewmen from the *Indemnity* last night, and we set a dozen fires and looted twenty shops. Did you know that they don't even lock their doors?"

Dudley nodded.

"I've arranged to stay on for a few days. I'm going to take a ground-floor office in a conspicuous location and get out some advertising circulars. We'll hit different neighborhoods tonight and tomorrow night, and after that you won't have to sell insurance. They'll come demanding it."

"You may be underestimating them."

"Nonsense. You take care of those claims, and then you get over to the northwest section and explain fire insurance to the people who had fires last night. I'll be looking for that new office. I'll meet you back here this evening."

"Right," Dudley said.

McGivern was waiting when Dudley returned to the apartment. He said quickly, "How'd you make out?"

Dudley seated himself wearily. "I *think* I've established an entirely new legal principle. And I'm worn out."

"You *think?* Is that the best you could do?"

"The judges are coming tonight to give me their verdict. I've been to the northwest section. Whatever you used to start those fires was darned effective."

"The *Indemnity's* engineering officer made some incendiary bombs. He could only get a dozen ready on short notice, but tonight there'll be twice as many."

"If you'd placed them carefully, you'd have had much better results," Dudley said.

"I suppose. We don't want to burn down the city, though —a small fire is better for our purposes than a large one." He chuckled. "It wouldn't do to burn so much that they have nothing left to insure."

"What'd you do with the stuff that was stolen?"

"It's stashed away on the *Indemnity*. We'll dump it as soon as we get into space."

"Then tonight you'll start twenty-four fires?"

"Right," McGivern said. "And we'll loot about fifty shops. Southwest section this time."

"And the new office?"

"Couldn't find anything I liked. I'll look again tomorrow. What is this legal principle you're working on?"

"I finally found out what was behind the Maylorian Rule of Justice. On this world the husband has to put up a sum of money that seems to be part dowry and part bride fee. The whole point in giving the violator's wife to the husband of the victim is that it supplies him with another wife without cost. Actually it's much more complicated than that, and the practice is encrusted with all manner of historical twists and precedences. What I'm trying to establish is that this is not a Rule of Justice—it's manifestly unjust because it breaks up a marriage and forces unknown and probably unwanted new spouses on the violator's wife and the victim's husband, who are innocent parties. The problem could be easily and justly solved by requiring the violator—or his insurance—to supply the marriage money so the husband of the victim can choose his own wife."

McGivern nodded thoughtfully. "If they accept it, we'll certainly have a basis for selling insurance."

Dudley said tiredly, "They've already accepted it on an optional basis. They're not ready to dump a time-tested social custom on the word of an Alien, but they're willing to let the victim's husband demand the price of a new wife in compensation if he prefers it that way. What I'm trying to get from them is a legal requirement that all groundcar drivers carry insurance —in the interest of justice."

McGivern's eyes bulged with excitement. "Gad! And Galactic is the only insurance company on Maylor!"

A knock sounded. "Want to hear the verdict?" Dudley asked.

"I can't wait."

Dudley opened the door and brought in the two judges and an escort of three police officers. The old judge muttered, "Tomorrow would have done just as well. I'll be late for dinner."

"Have you reached a decision, Your Wisdom?" Dudley asked.

"We have. Your petition is granted. Settlement in the two cases in which you are involved shall be as you requested, and we take note of your generous offer to accept a token settlement from the workman whose clumsiness killed your wife. Your petition is also granted as to the insurance requirement, which will be presented to the Council tomorrow, along with the charter application of the Maylorian Insurance Company."

"*Maylorian* Insurance Company?" McGivern exclaimed.

"Thank you, Your Wisdom," Dudley said. "Did you record in full the conversation that took place while you were waiting?"

The judge sighed. "We did. We found it difficult to believe, but the facts you have revealed to us support it completely. We accept your recommendations. The charter of the Galactic Insurance Company will be revoked tomorrow. Clearance will be denied Alien McGivern's yacht until the stolen articles are returned and compensation paid for the fire damage. We will arrange with the Interplanetary Authority to securely incarcerate him at the port until justice has been fulfilled. Is this satisfactory?"

"Perfectly satisfactory," Dudley said. "I'd like a few words in private with Alien McGivern, and then you can have him."

"Certainly."

Dudley closed the door after them. It was the first time he'd ever been able to face McGivern without being afraid of him, and he'd looked forward to the moment with pleasure. The expected blast of anger did not materialize, however. McGivern said quietly, "You're out of your mind."

"On the contrary, the longer I stay on Maylor, the saner I seem to get."

"I suppose you realize that you're fired."

"I've already sent my resignation to the *Indemnity.*"

"I won't accept it. You're fired. I feel a little sorry for you, Dudley. You've ruined what might have been a brilliant career. You'll never hold another job with an insurance company—I can promise you that."

"I already have one," Dudley said. "You're speaking with the new president of the about-to-be-chartered Maylorian Insurance Company. Since I'll have an absolute monopoly of this world's business, I expect to do rather well. I also expect to evolve an insurance industry aimed at serving the people instead of itself."

"If there was a psychiatrist available, I'd have you examined," McGivern said bitterly. "But I don't suppose this damned planet has one."

"Today," Dudley said, "for the first time in my entire career, you gave me your wholehearted approval for something I'd done. After we parted, I got to wondering what sort of an accomplishment that was when it required the calloused exploitation of a double murder to bring it about. Up to that moment I certainly needed a psychiatrist, but since then I've made a remarkable improvement. Perhaps it's the result of associating with people who aren't greedy or afraid and who have healthy minds." He smiled complacently. "They're so grateful for this exposure of the infamous Galactic Insurance plot that they've given me a public appointment. I'm a member of a committee charged with the guardianship of public morals and customs, and I've already squelched the recommendation by an alien engineer that Maylor City install one-way streets and traffic lanes."

McGivern glared at him, tightlipped.

"I'm not—really—being *too* ruthless," Dudley murmured as he turned him over to the police.

They took McGivern away, and Dudley left immediately afterward and walked through the crush of rush-hour traffic toward the restaurant where Bakr had taken them that first night. The atmosphere would be sterile, and the food would be disgustingly bland, and this time Dudley expected to enjoy it.